# SWEET TIDINGS

## INDIGO BAY CHRISTMAS ROMANCES

## JEAN C. GORDON

UPSTATE NY ROMANCE

# SWEET TIDINGS

Amanda Strickland wants her first Christmas as mayor of Indigo Bay to be a civic success from the animal shelter fundraiser to benefit gala to the traditional tree lighting. And movie-star acquaintance Eric Slade may be just the ingredient she needs to pull it all off.

Eric wants to put the paparazzi off him and the young co-star of his last film—and protect his fragile relationship with the grown son he never spent much time with when his son was growing up. When he proposes a pretend holiday romance between him and Amanda, it seems like a win-win for them both.

But what will happen when the pretend romance turns real and snafus on both sides threaten to crush their Christmas plans and hearts?

Sweet Tidings is the first book in the new Indigo

Bay Christmas Romances Series, but it and the other stories are standalone and can be read in any order.

"What is the Indigo Bay Christmas Romances series? It's a continuation of the popular Indigo Bay Sweet Romance and Second Chance Romance series with tons of fun for readers! But more specifically, it's a set of books written by authors who love romance. Grab a mug of hot chocolate, drop into a comfy chair, and get ready to be swept away into this charming South Carolina beach town.

The Indigo Bay world has been written so readers can dive in anywhere in the series without missing a beat. Read one or all—they're all sweet, fun rides that you won't soon forget. Also, as special treats, you'll see some recurring characters. How many can you find?

Sweet Tidings by Jean C. Gordon

Sweet Noel by Jeanette Lewis
Sweet Joymaker by Jean Oram
Sweet Yuletide by Melissa McClone
Sweet Mistletoe by Elizabeth Bromke
Sweet Carol by Shanae Johnson

Find out more about Indigo Bay at
www.sweetreadbooks.com/indigo-bay

Much thanks to my critique group BFF (Colleen, Chris, and Thomasine), my editor Jena O'Connor, my cover designer, Najla Qamber, and last but not least, the Sweet Reads author group for inviting me to visit Indigo Bay again with them. I couldn't have done it without you all."

# CHAPTER 1

The gates of his Calabasas estate closed behind him. If anyone was following him, they wouldn't get in. It was good to know he still had it. But this woman—girl if he was honest—pursuing him was too much. Even for him, Eric Slade, action adventure movie star with a reputation of chasing almost anything in skirts. He drove up the winding driveway to the house and slapped the steering wheel when he spied the starlet's car parked there —again.

Eric pulled his Jag into the garage. Finding her here alone was better than her and her phalanx of media people showing up wherever he went in public. His son Chris denied letting Maya London in the gates, and he thought he trusted his small staff not to. Eric rubbed the back of his neck. Unless Chris was busting on him. In collusion with Maya. Acting out, setting him up in retaliation for all the times he'd stood his son up for a woman. Eric dragged himself out of the car and walked toward the house.

Maya burst out of the house, ran down the path and hurled herself at him. A man jumped out from behind a hedge and flashed a picture. Eric pushed her away. "Out. Off my property."

Maya gave him her signature pout, the one that served her so well as the latest starlet to join him in one of his adventure movies.

"If I find you here again, I'm calling the police and signing a restraining order." His lawyer had told him to do as much. But the girl could act. They had online chemistry, and he didn't want to rule out using her in any of his future films.

She stalked to her car. "Chris said it was okay if I waited inside for you."

The photographer slinked to the other side of the car.

"Go," he roared and went inside once her taillights disappeared down the driveway. Eric checked the gate camera to make sure she was out and locked the gate. He rubbed his forehead. He didn't want to believe it was Chris. The two of them had been finding their way back to father and son since Chris had gotten out of the military and come to live in one of guest cottages here while going to Loyola Law School. His son had even agreed to spend Christmas together, but that could have been because his ex-wife, Chris's mother, was spending the holiday in Paris with husband number three.

Eric's cell phone rang and he took it out of his pocket to see a familiar number. "Hey, Jeff," he greeted his childhood and still best friend.

"Eric, I know you're a busy man, but give me a little help here. Sonja's after me to get your answer about Christmas."

"Ah, so some of the gold's wearing off," Eric teased.

"Not in the least," Jeff retorted. "But it would make my life easier if she didn't keep asking me to get an answer out of you."

"Okay, I'll put you out of your misery. Chris…" he crossed his fingers, "and I are coming. We'll take the B&B suite if no one else has already reserved it."

"Nope, we've saved it for you, our treat."

"Not a chance. I'll pay the full holiday price."

Silence filled the airwaves. He'd done it again. Insulted someone, his best friend, with his boastful attitude toward money. Chris had certainly pointed out that fault of his enough times.

"I mean," Eric dived in to save himself and save Jeff face. "I'd like to do that as my Christmas gift to you and Sonja. Saves me having to come up with something."

"In that case, maybe she should charge you double."

"Don't get carried away." Eric leaned his shoulder

against the wall and thought of the peacefulness of Indigo Bay, South Carolina, where Jeff's wife and son ran the Mansion B&B. That thought was followed by another. One that should solve his problem with Maya and be enjoyable, very enjoyable in the process.

"Okay, then, I'll tell Sonja you and Chris are on for the holiday, coming when?"

"What about today?"

"Fine with me. I've got an old Harley I'm tinkering with that you could help me with. But I'm not sure the suite is available. I'd have to check."

"As long as you have a room, I'm good. I'll text you my arrival time in Charleston."

"Do that, and I'll be there."

"Later," Eric signed off. He buzzed his pilot and arranged for his plane to be ready Then, cracking a grin, he scrolled down his contact list to put his other thought into action.

MAYOR AMANDA STRICKLAND slapped her desk. She held a Master's degree in planning for heaven's sake. So why was planning the Indigo Bay Christmas season getting to her? Three perfectly good reasons. She could tick them off like items in a to-do list. It was her first Christmas as Indigo Bay's mayor. She wanted to do right by her adopted hometown that she loved. And because she was a perfectionist.

Her phone rang. "Hello, Mayor Strickland," she answered with her title as usual.

"Well, hello Mayor Strickland."

It took Amanda a moment to identify the deep drawl on the other end. "Well, as I live and breathe," she said in her best southern belle imitation. "Is this movie mogul, Eric Slade?"

Eric laughed. "The one and only."

Amanda went back to her normal voice. "To what do I owe the honor?"

"I have a proposition."

His words sent a shiver through her that they shouldn't. They'd worked together during the last hurricane to hit Indigo Bay and usually went out to dinner or something whenever he was in town visiting Jeff and Sonja Brewster. Purely as friends. Anything more would be beyond what she'd want to handle. A disastrous secret engagement back in grad school had resulted in her mom giving her a piece of advice she followed to this day. Too bad her mom hadn't taken it herself.

"What will Maya London think?" She shook her head. Why had she said that? It was admitting that she at least read the tabloid magazines' headlines in store checkout lines. Which she did, and always had, although she wasn't in the habit of buying them. Except on the occasions when the headline mentioned him.

"Hopefully, that I'm unavailable, no matter how

much she stalks me," he answered in a resigned voice.

"She's been stalking you?"

"What else could it be? She's young enough to be my daughter."

Amanda gulped a breath. She'd insulted him. "Sorry, I'm kind of stressed. What are you thinking?"

"I'm spending the holidays with Jeff and Sonja. "My thought is we hang out like we usually do, but make it look like a little more. Then, an amicable split after the holidays."

"A fake holiday romance? Have you been watching Hallmark Christmas movies?

"Hallmark? No!"

Amanda couldn't determine whether his denial was pure disgust or a too emphatic protest. "I'm going to have to give your proposition some thought and let you know. Either way, I'm looking forward to seeing you again." If her breathlessness was any indication, a little too much.

"I'll have to be satisfied with that. But it could be fun. Even mayors are allowed to have fun."

If the last six months were any indication, she'd be inclined to say no. Maybe it was time for some fun. "I'll let you know," she repeated before she agreed on impulse. She had a lot on her mayoral plate right now. "Bye."

No sooner had Amanda hung up than the phone

rang again. Her heartbeat quickened and she steeled herself against another onslaught from Eric.

"Amanda, your mother called," the city officials administrative assistant said.

"Thanks, Tracy. I'll give her a call back."

Amanda clicked off. Another reason her social life had become a dessert. The death of her birth father, whom she hadn't met until her mother had reunited with him six years ago and moved to Indigo Bay. Her chest tightened. For much of that time, his health had been failing and her mother had devoted her time to caring for him. Now, Mom had little to do.

"Hi, Mom," she said when her mother answered on the first ring.

"Amanda, the kid didn't come mow like he was supposed to."

Empathy at the depth of her mother's loss warred with irritation that this was what her 58-year-old mother who'd independently marched through life until six years ago had become. "Why don't you go next door and find out why? Maybe he forgot."

"I won't be imposing?"

"No. You hired him for a job. He didn't show. If you'd rather call, I have his number." As did Mom.

"Maybe you could …" Her mother started.

"No," Amanda interrupted. "I have work to do here and more at my business office afterwards."

"I suppose I could go over," her mother said before saying goodbye.

Amanda could only hope the neighbor was home and possibly would invite her mother in for coffee and talk. She went back to checking email, putting aside one from Lucille Sanderson, who was somewhat of a community character, for last. The others were reports from various people working on community holiday events. She read the reports first and then tackled the last two emails. One was Lucille's and the other a report that a streetlamp was out on one of the residential streets. She assured the sender that the highway department would be on the light and leaned back in her chair to enjoy Lucille's email.

Ah, this week's complaint was about the dog park. Amanda laughed aloud. People were not cleaning up after their pets properly, and Lucille had almost ruined her ruby sparkle sandals. The one's that match her dog Princess's ruby sparkle collar. Amanda assured the senior citizen that she'd talk to the police chief and ask him if any of his patrols could fit in an additional drive-by of the dog park.

Almost immediately, she received an email from the chief saying that Indigo Bay certainly couldn't have Lucille's sandals ruined. What would she wear on ruby sparkle day?

With that done, Amanda took off her mayor's hat and closed the office. She let the administrative assistant know she was gone for the day and left for her architectural office a few blocks away. The walk in the brisk December air cleared her mind of most of her mayoral duties but left a wide space for weighing Eric's proposition. She arrived at her architectural office with the pros and cons of agreeing evenly balanced. She left a few hours later no closer to a decision.

Then, on her way home to her beachside cottage, she hit on a decider.

ERIC SCANNED the waiting area of the Charleston airport. His pilot had gotten a good tailwind and they'd arrived early. He hadn't texted Jeff because his friend was always early. Always, except today. He dropped his luggage by a seat and pulled his baseball cap lower, keeping his head down. No one had recognized him. Generally, he didn't mind a little fan appreciation, but Maya London and her random surprise appearances were fast changing that. He tensed when he sensed rather than saw someone approaching.

When he saw a pair of wedges displaying toenails polished in hot pink, his head shot up. Maya couldn't have followed him here.

"Surprise!"

He nearly choked but recovered quickly. "Why Mayor Strickland," he drawled, as he stood and faced her, thinking she was one fine looking woman.

"I almost didn't recognize you." Eric nodded at her toes. "And your hair. It's longer and lighter."

"Nor I you." Amanda raised an eyebrow, as she stroked her chin.

Eric imitated her, stroking his chin beard. "That's right, I didn't have this the last time I was here. What do you think?"

"Nice."

"The white strands aren't too much?" Okay, so he had been looking for a compliment, but now he sounded just plain needy.

"That depends," she answered.

"On what?"

"Whether they're natural or salon created."

"You wound me. I didn't ask about your hair."

She laughed. He'd forgotten how much he liked that genuine sound.

He put his hand to his heart. "Of course they're natural. So natural my agent wants me to have them touched up dark. She thinks they make me look old."

"Distinguished," Amanda said. "And I freely admit I've had a few highlights added to my hair."

"I'll tell her that. The distinguished part." He picked up his luggage. "Lead away while you tell me why you're here to pick me up instead of Jeff. Or can I speculate good tidings?"

"You can speculate all you want. I've been thinking about your proposition all day, including on my drive here."

So she hadn't planned the pickup to let him down in person, the first thought he'd had when he'd recognized her.

"And, drumroll, the decision is?"

She stopped by an SUV in the short-term parking and unlocked the hatch for his luggage, staying right where she was.

He moved close to place his bags in the car. She was killing him.

Amanda closed the hatch and a slow smile spread across her lips. Her hot-pink tinted lips.

"I'm in," she said, striding away to the driver's side door."

His heart soared far more than he'd expected. Eric used his steps to the passenger side to recover his equilibrium. So overwhelmed he forgot to wonder what was in it for her. *Hollywood.*

"You didn't tell Jeff why you wanted to pick me up, did you?"

"Of course not. I told him you'd let me know you were coming, and I haven't seen you in a while."

"He didn't act suspicious? I did tell him about Maya and wanting to get out of Dodge when I called him about coming earlier than I'd planned."

"No, although he got one of those smug man-looks on his face," Amanda said.

"Really?" So his friend must think he was putting the moves on her. Or, better, her on him.

"Yes, really. And if you keep grilling me, I could change my mind."

"Done." He snapped his mouth shut and raised his hands in surrender.

"Like you said, it should be fun. Our own little Christmas secret. You won't have trouble keeping it, will you? People's respect for me as mayor could be damaged if the ruse got out."

"The secret? Of course not." He ran his gaze over the beautiful, interesting woman sitting next to him.

The pretend part, on the other hand, was cracking right before his eyes.

# CHAPTER 2

The phone woke Amanda from a deep sleep that her alarm had failed to. A sleep she'd achieved finally in the early hours of the morning. She had only 20 minutes to get to work. Not that she had to punch a time-clock at city hall, but she worked best on a regular schedule.

She glanced at her cell phone. The Mansion B&B. Amanda debated letting it ring. She wasn't sure she was ready to face Eric yet today, even if it was only over the phone. Her finger punched answer anyway.

"Amanda?"

It was Sonja. "Hi."

"I'm glad I caught you before you left."

"What's up?" Amanda rolled out of bed and took the outfit she'd planned for today out of her closet.

"We have a problem here at the B&B. The plumbing to the suite Eric's staying in is backed up.

Jeff thinks it's something with the outflow to the city sewer line."

Amanda put her phone on speaker so she could dress. "Have you called the Public Works Department?" She'd never figured out why people were so quick to call the mayor for problems that other city departments covered.

"That's not it." Sonja corrected. "We have a plumber coming to check our line and will call Public Works if it's something beyond our responsibility."

"Oh." Amanda went to work on her makeup. "Then, what's the problem?"

"We don't have any rooms Eric can move into."

Amanda wasn't exactly following. "So you want me to ask around at city hall about places that may have openings?" It was all she could think of.

"No, we have an idea. You're friends …"

"He can't stay here. It wouldn't look right." She pulled her hair back into a French twist.

"Right. That's not our idea. Jeff and I were thinking of your mother's place, only until the suite's plumbing is fixed. She has all that room, and I know you're concerned about her not getting out and socializing as she used to."

"Maybe. It would give her someone to look after. I'll ask her."

"Thanks. Eric said he has things to do this morning."

"Okay, I'll check with her this morning and let you know."

"Great. I'll let you go." Sonja hung up.

Amanda gave the clock a final glance. If she drove, she could be to city hall by 9:00.

Tracy waylaid her in the hall to the mayor's office. "Eric Slade. The movie star Eric Slade is waiting for you in your office."

"Thank you," Amanda said as if having movie stars drop in on her was an everyday occurrence, which it could be until Christmas. She smiled and walked into her office.

"Hi," he said, rising from his seat. "Did Sonja call you?"

"She did." Amana walked to her desk. Eric had gone super casual today. A black t-shirt and jeans. Somehow that made him look younger, despite the sprinkle of white in his beard. Her mind went randomly to the thought that she didn't know how old he was, except he had to be older than her 38. "I haven't talked with Mom yet. It might be better if we went over to her house and talked with her in person."

"Sure." He sat again and motioned her to her desk. "But first, we have some unfinished business."

She pursed her lips and sat. "What?"

"I know what you're doing as part of our deal. I want to do something in return."

"You could couch-surf your stay in Indigo Bay for

donations to the animal shelter's fundraiser with each night going to the highest bidder."

Eric made a choking sound. "Sorry. I do surf, but I haven't done that variety in 20 years."

She laughed. "I'm kidding. How about taking me to the Barks and Bows Gala the Saturday before Christmas to raise funds for the Indigo Bay Animal Shelter?"

"Nice name. And easy request. But you have to let me buy the tickets."

The picture that flashed in her mind of what Eric would look like in a tux took her breath away. "I'm not done," she got out in an almost normal voice. "The shelter is having tours with a delayed-adoption clinic the Tuesday after the gala. The pets won't go to their new homes until after Christmas. You can help me staff the time slot I signed up for, assuming you don't have any pet allergies." The man had to have some physical imperfection.

"No allergies, and the adoption clinic would be a perfect progression in our Hallmark romance."

"And a crowd draw, I would think."

"Of course, who wouldn't want to meet Madam Mayor in person."

She gave him a wry smile. "There is that."

Eric rose. "Let me know when you're free to go talk with your mother about my lodging."

Amanda checked her desk calendar. She didn't

have anything scheduled. "We could go now."
Something in her was unwilling to let him go.

"Tracy said you have office hours until noon."

He was on a first name basis with her
administrative assistant. Of course he was. "I have
nothing pressing this morning, and Tracy knows how
to reach me if she needs to."

When she stepped around her desk. Eric gave her
a once-over, lingering on her pencil skirt. "I
borrowed one of Jeff's bikes."

"And I'm not exactly dressed for a motorcycle
ride. No problem. Mom lives close. We can walk."

"Walk it is." He waited for her and took her hand.
She gently disentangled it. "Not in city hall."

"You're the boss."

Somehow, she thought few people bossed Eric
Slade, at least not more than once.

At the sidewalk in front of city hall, Amanda
slipped her fingers between his. She might as well
take advantage of the opportunity to be the boss and
lead him around while she had it. And the firm grip
of his hand wasn't a bad perk either.

AMANDA'S GRIP on his hand felt good and, to him,
said a lot about her. She was a woman who was used
to being in charge, who had a definite life of her own.
A woman he'd genuinely like to get to know better,

unlike anyone he'd been with or dated in a long time. They'd generally been using him as much or more than he'd been using them.

He swallowed hard. That was sort of what their fake romance was. He shook his head. No theirs was a mutually beneficial agreement. But wasn't that what a lot of his relationships had been? Call it what he might, it was still the same Hollywood game. You scratch my back; I'll scratch yours.

"What?" Amanda interrupted his thoughts. "You shook your head."

"Nothing. I was thinking."

"Me, too. There's a lot I don't know about the real you."

He scoffed. "You might be better not knowing."

"I mean ordinary things people who are dating know."

"All right, ask me something."

"How old are you?"

He hesitated, glancing sideways at her. Amanda couldn't be older than her mid-30s.

"It's not a trick question."

"Forty-two."

"Your IMBd says 45."

He puffed out a breath. "Okay 48. And up until five months ago, I smoked cigarettes." That brought a grin to her face that quickly faded.

"Don't tell my mother."

"About smoking?"

"No, your age."

He cocked his head. "Why? Does she have a thing about you dating older men. I'd think you're beyond having parental rules on your dating."

Amanda frowned. "Of course I'm beyond that. I have had a thing against dating significantly older men. A disaster with an instructor in grad school."

This was probably where he should change the subject, but it was just getting interesting. "What's significantly older?"

She shrugged before she shot out, "Ten years."

"How old are you?"

"Thirty-eight," she said as she turned the corner onto a residential street of stately old homes.

"Hmm. When's your birthday?"

"What does …"

"Humor me."

"July."

He breathed an exaggerated sigh of relief. "Mine is in September, so I'm not ten years older than you. Problem solved."

Amanda slowed her pace to almost a crawl as they approached the only home on the street so far that didn't have a perfectly groomed front lawn. "My father—sperm donor, really—was 15 years older than my mother. I first met him six years ago when he and my mother reconnected after his wife's death."

She stopped talking. He waited. Eric knew Amanda had moved to Indigo Bay and opened her architectural and planning consulting firm about that time. She'd told him her mother had lured her there with talk of the delights of small-town beach living.

"He had terminable cancer. Mom gave up everything she'd built for herself. She was career military. And she moved back to Indigo Bay, her hometown, to take care of him. I gave her a hard time, a really hard time about it. Coming here to take care of that old man who'd had nothing to do with us for all that time."

Eric could almost taste the bitterness in Amanda's words. "How long did he live?"

"He hung on for four and a half years, until he'd drained everything out of Mom."

Eric knew this was dangerous ground, but he needed to know Amanda as much as possible. For their charade, of course. "I take it you two never reconciled."

She stopped short at the end of the next driveway. "He never acknowledged me. He only wanted Mom." She cleared her throat and motioned to the house. "We're here. It looks like Mom didn't talk with the teen next door who was supposed to have mowed her lawn yesterday."

A woman came to the front screen door. She opened it as Amanda called, "Hi," and walked him up the driveway to the walk leading to the wraparound front porch.

"Amanda, you should have called first," the

woman scolded in a voice that had a much-more-pronounced South Carolina accent than Amanda's. "The house is a mess."

"I'm sure it's fine," Eric assured her as he took in the woman. He could see where Amanda got her looks from. But her mother looked older than he'd expected. Amanda had told him before that her mother was barely out of her teens when she'd had her.

"No, it's not," the elder Ms. Strickland said. At least he assumed it was Ms. Strickland. Amanda hadn't said anything about her parents marrying.

He almost missed Amanda's slight nod as her mother sized him up much as he had her. He scratched an itch on his forearm. Did Amanda mean yes, the house was a mess or no her mother was just saying that?

"You and your friend can sit on the porch and I'll bring us all some sweet tea to drink while you tell me why you're here."

"We might as well take the swing and get the neighborhood talking," Amanda said.

She settled on the swing, and he sat appropriately close with his arm on the backrest behind her. "Your mother doesn't know who I am, does she?"

"Oh yeah, she does, and for some reason she isn't happy about it."

"Oh, I didn't read that at all."

Amanda raised an eyebrow.

"And here I thought I was pretty experienced in reading women."

Amanda patted his knee, causing him to squeeze the swing's padded back rather that her shoulder he wanted to squeeze.

She left her hand on his knee. "Don't worry, Mom's opinion won't affect our dea…plans." She changed her wording as they heard the screen door creak open and left her hand on his knee while taking her glass of tea with the other hand.

Amanda's mother's gaze remained fixed on her daughter's hand while handing him his drink. Then, as she moved to sit down, her gaze went to the magazine holder sitting between the swing and her chair. One of the popular tabloid magazines with a face she was currently very familiar with leered from the cover.

"Mom!" Amanda took the magazine from the holder. "You don't buy this magazine?"

"Certainly not. Lucille and I trade magazines. That must have been in the ones she brought me. So, you must have a reason for taking off work to come here."

"Yes, but first where are my manners? Mom, this is Eric Slade. Eric, my mother, Lisa Strickland."

"Nice to meet you, Ms. Strickland" he said with his most photogenic smile.

"You can call me Lisa."

That was something. Although Amanda's earlier

suggestion about couch-surfing for animal-shelter donations was looking more attractive.

AMANDA GLANCED from Eric to her mother and back. This was going well—not. She removed her hand from Eric's knee, and he dropped his arm to her shoulders. Give me a break. She reminded herself that this was for charity and took a cleansing breath. "Eric is here visiting Jeff and Sonja for the holidays. But they have a plumbing problem in the suite he's booked and have so other rooms available while the problem is getting fixed."

"I see." Her mother looked at Eric's arm, frowned, and said, "He can't stay with you. You're the mayor. How would that look?"

"Exactly what I thought," Eric said.

Her mother's expression remained the same. Amanda wasn't sure he was helping matters, particularly with the way the corners of his mouth were twitching. "Yes, Sonja suggested I ask you if Eric could stay here. You have lots of room."

"I don't know …"

"I'll pay you what I'm paying for the B&B suite," Eric offered.

Amanda rubbed her forehead. Wrong again. Mom was likely to take that as meaning she needed financial help. As long as Amanda could remember,

Mom had prided herself at being able to take care of herself—and Amanda, too, when she was growing up.

"I don't need you to pay me," her mother said right on cue.

"I wouldn't feel right not doing something to reciprocate." Eric looked at the lawn and the house. "Do you have anything that needs to be done around the house and grounds?"

"There are a few things. I don't know if you could handle them."

Amanda stared at her feet. But, when she looked up, Eric didn't appear the least bit insulted.

"I wasn't always an actor. I worked construction summers while I was going to college and when I first started my acting career. It could help me get back in shape."

Amanda felt his muscled thigh resting along hers. He looked in good shape to her. "Eric still does his own movie stunts," she blurted for whatever reason.

"Some of them," he clarified.

"All right. You can stay here until your suite at the B&B is ready. Give me a little time to clean up the house before you bring your things over."

"Thanks. Should I bring lunch, too?" he asked.

"No. I'll fix something."

Eric placed his hand over Amanda's on her leg. "You going to join us for lunch?"

Did she detect desperation in his voice and touch?

She smiled to herself. "Sorry, I've lost a good part of my morning at city hall. I'll send out for something and eat at my desk." She placed her empty tea glass on the porch next to the swing. "It'll give you two a chance to get to know each other." And give me a break from both of you.

Eric pushed the swing back to stand and caught Amanda off-guard. Her foot hit her glass, which rolled toward her mother who bent and scooped it up.

"Amanda Jade," her mother admonished.

One corner of Eric's mouth quirked up, and Amanda was hard-pressed not to smile back.

"You know those are the glasses from your grandmother's house. I only have the four of them."

Eric rose and handed his glass to her mother with a slight bow.

"Suck-up," she said in a soft voice he may or may not have heard, rising to stand beside him.

"Hell-oo."

All three of them looked toward the sidewalk to Lucille and Princess now making their way up the driveway.

Amanda's stomach dropped. She'd lost enough of her office time already and might have to make her consulting call from city hall, mixing governing with business. Something she didn't like to do or see anyone else doing.

"I couldn't tell from the street who you had with

you, Amanda. But my stars, it's Eric Slade," she said from the bottom of the porch stairs.

"Come up and meet him," Amanda said.

"Can you take Princess? The steps are a little steep."

"I will." Eric reached down and took the little dog. He glanced from the dog's bejeweled collar to Lucille's matching heels and went down the steps to give Lucille an arm up, as well.

"Such a gentleman," Lucille gushed.

"Yes, he is." Both Lucille and Eric were blocking her only escape route unless she leaped over the porch rail to the lawn.

"But a naughty one." Lucille nodded toward the magazine holder. "I hope you're not going to play with our Amanda's affections. What are your intentions?"

Eric handed Princess back to Lucille. "I intend to spend as much time as I can while I'm here getting to know her better."

Lucille looked at him approvingly.

Her mother lifted her eyebrows.

Eric assumed a self-satisfied Cheshire Cat smile.

And Amanda wanted to be alone in her office, planning for a successful town holiday season. Not to mention thinking through the serious doubts she had now about pulling off their romance charade.

How could she have left the good citizens of Indigo Bay of her simple list of pros and cons?

# CHAPTER 3

Amanda had declined his offer to walk her back to city hall, leaving him with the two older women. On closer look, and in contrast to Lucille, Lisa appeared younger than he'd initially thought. The salt and pepper hair had thrown him off. The age span between Lisa and him might not be much more than that between Amanda and him.

"What do you think, Eric?" Lucille asked.

"Hmm?" He had no idea what the women had been talking about.

"Ah, young love. No matter," Lucille said.

Eric worked at stifling a choke. He hadn't felt young in a while. At least not since the start of his last movie with the 24-year-old Maya as his co-star and the suggestion by his co-producer that he do fewer of his own stunts.

Princess whined at Lucille's feet. "We have to get going," she said. "Care to escort me?"

"Sure." About as much as the bath in boiling oil his character had escaped in one of his early films. "I'll see you later, Lisa. And thanks again."

Amanda's mother nodded and went inside.

"So," Lucille said when they reached the front sidewalk. "I hope this isn't a rebound fling you're planning with our Amanda."

"I'm not sure I follow." Neither what she said or the possessive "our Amanda." He wasn't up on small-town peculiarities. Did people other than Lucille think their mayor personally belonged to them? He'd have to run that by Jeff.

"You can be honest with me. I'll keep my lips sealed. A rebound romance from Maya London's breakup? The latest tabloid headlines," she prompted.

He rubbed the back of his neck and reminded himself that it would be rude for him to break into a jog. "What are the magazines saying?"

"Not too much, but she's been photographed out with an unidentified…" Lucille hesitated. "Younger man."

He touched her shoulder. "You've made my day."

"You're welcome. I think."

They'd reached the city hall parking lot. "It was nice meeting you and Princess," he said, petting the dog before he strode off toward the bike Jeff had lent him. He glanced at the window he'd determined was Amanda's office. His PR people would be proud of him. They were always telling him to keep people guessing about his so-called private life. He had Lucille guessing, and Amanda, too, he hoped. Keep her interested.

"Hey," Sonja said from the front desk when he walked into the B&B a couple minutes later. "All your city hall business taken care of?"

Eric didn't remember saying anything about city hall when he'd left earlier. "Business, and I had the pleasure of meeting Lucille and Princess at Amanda's mother's place. She's a fan—Lucille, not Princess."

"You don't know. Princess could be, too. You didn't ask?" She didn't wait for an answer. "I'm surprised you haven't met her when you've visited before."

"Just lucky, I guess."

Sonja laughed.

"Is Jeff around? I need to borrow his truck to drive my stuff over to Lisa Strickland's house."

"I'm glad she agreed. It'll be good for her to have some life in that place. It was Amanda's father's place, and I don't think Lisa has changed a thing since she moved in."

"She took me up on an offer to do some work around the place."

"Even better." Sonja pulled a set of keys from behind the counter. "Take my car. Jeff is working with the plumber in the basement right now, and I'm not sure you—or anyone—wants to interrupt that."

She tossed him the keys. "Hopefully, you'll be able to clear out your things before they come up."

"Thanks, on both counts." Eric was well aware of the dangers of working with Jeff when something wasn't going according to plans, as he suspected the plumbing job wasn't.

Upstairs, he decided to grab all his stuff, since he hadn't really unpacked it last night. A thud and a yell echoed from below as he stepped down into the front room again. And who knew how long he might be staying at Lisa's?

"What are you doing for lunch?" Sonja asked, following a metal against metal bang this time.

"Lisa invited me. I'm not sure I know her well enough yet to bring a plus one."

"That's okay. My escaping here until Jeff and the plumber are done is only wishful thinking. Someone has to cover the desk. Maybe, I can get him over to the motorcycle shop this afternoon. Weren't the two of you going to work on something there?"

"Yeah, he has an old Harley and the scooter he's helping a guy fix up for some Christmas giveaway lined up." His phone pinged. He read the text. "That was Guaranteed Delivery. My bike is arriving this afternoon. I'm having it delivered to the shop. I assume someone is there who can sign for it."

"No problem. The shop is open."

"If you need to get him out of the house tomorrow, I want Jeff to help with a tune-up and a few other things on my bike. I'll talk with him later about it."

"Good. Maybe the plumber will be done by then. Or even today if I can get Jeff to let the man do his job."

"I'll bring your car back as soon as I can."

"Whenever. I'm not going anywhere. Will we see you for supper?"

"I'm leaving myself open. I'll let you know."

Sonja smiled. "More city hall business?"

Eric just grinned and waved bye. He whistled his way to the car. Sonja already had suspicions about him and Amanda. He was quite sure Lucille wouldn't be keeping as quiet as she'd said. If he could get a picture of him and Amanda, he could send it anonymously to the president of his fan club…

This was even easier than he'd thought it would be.

~

"Need a lift?" The question pulled Amanda out of her mental list of things for the holiday festivities that she hadn't gotten to today. She glanced at Sonja's car rolling along beside her. But it hadn't been Sonja's voice. Nor was it Sonja driving. She stopped. The car stopped.

She walked to the open passenger side window. "I'm just going to my other office." She pointed at the building behind her. "I need to make a couple of calls. I don't like to mix private business with mayoral business."

"Will it take long? I have a favor to ask."

She'd spent a good part of the morning with him. She shouldn't give him her afternoon, too. She had to establish some limits to their charade. "Not more than a half hour." Evidently her mouth hadn't checked with her brain. "What's the favor?"

"I need to pick my bike up. I had it shipped to Jeff's shop. If you could drive Sonja's car back to the B&B, you'd save her or Jeff having to drive me later to pick it up."

"As if you couldn't walk back and get the bike." Her attempt at a stern face didn't last long before she broke into a smile.

"Maybe I'm trying to impress you. Get you on my bike, arms wrapped around me for a ride to city hall afterwards to pick up your car. Isn't that what men do to woo women?"

She laughed. "I'm still wrapping my mind around your shipping your motorcycle from California for vacation." And recovering full strength in my knees after the thought of my arms wrapped around you.

Her dating life had definitely been in far too long of a dry spell if Eric's words had affected her that much.

"What do you say?" Eric assumed a puppy dog look.

"Yes, if it will put an end to the bad acting. I'll meet you at Jeff's shop when I'm done."

"Great, I'll hang out there and wait for you." He checked his mirror and took off faster than necessary, but at least he didn't make the tires squeal.

Amanda unlocked her office. She was going to have to talk with him about toning down the teen crush behavior. That wasn't how she pictured their holiday charade. She saw something more elegant, with the gala, and more sedate. Something like walking Seaside Boulevard and the board walk in the moonlight taking in the stores' and businesses' Christmas decorations. Maybe a little holiday shopping together. Quiet dinners in the places they'd be most likely to be seen. Eric standing with her at the traditional Indigo Bay Christmas lighting.

She sat at her desk. That reminded her. She should tell him about the other tradition of hanging an ornament on the tree before the lighting. And she should get her calls made. Amanda picked up her phone. After playing a little telephone tag, it was almost an hour before she left for Seaside Cycles.

Her steps quickened the closer she got and not just because she was later than she'd said. She had to admit that she was also anxious to step into her role as Eric Slade's holiday romance.

"Hi, Ms. Strickland," Liam, the college student who worked for Jeff said.

"Hi, I'm supposed to meet Eric… Eric Slade here." Shish, what other Eric could she be meeting?

"He's in the back. Through the red door," Liam finished with an almost smirk.

"Thanks." A qualm traveled from her chest to her stomach and back. Was that how people were going to react to her and Eric? As if she didn't know what she was getting into? No. Liam was barely out of his teens. Not representative of Indigo Bay's electorate at large.

When she entered the back room, Eric was crouched beside a motorcycle so engrossed in what he was doing that he didn't notice her. She took the opportunity to study him. His classic profile, nicely muscled arm wielding a wrench, broad shoulders, and still narrow waist—despite the hint of love handles. He moved, and she stopped her perusal.

"Hi, sorry it took me longer than I expected."

He rose and rubbed his hands on a cloth he pulled out of his back pocket. "No, perfect timing. It took me longer than I'd expected to get everything in running order. What do you think?"

What was she supposed to say? "It's big and shiny."

His laughed emphasized the crinkles at the corners of his eyes. "Yes, it is."

"Loud, too, I suspect."

"No louder than allowed by the California Department of Motor Vehicles regulations. I didn't check the South Carolina ones."

"I think you're safe, here in Indigo Bay at least. Our police force may be more likely to ask you for your autograph on a ticket than write you one."

"Whew!" He made an exaggerated show of wiping his forehead. "I'll clean up. Then we can go."

"Sure."

He headed to the storefront.

Amanda walked around the motorcycle and ran her fingertip over the logo on the gas tank. A name she didn't recognize. But then, she didn't know anything about motorcycles.

"All set." He came back carrying two helmets. "I know South Carolina doesn't require them, but I'm used to wearing one and thought you'd want to."

"Definitely." And maybe some body armor. "But I thought I was driving Sonja's car."

"You are. It's in the municipal parking lot. I'll drive you to it."

Amanda swallowed. "Is this where I tell you I've never ridden on a motorcycle before?" *Never particularly wanted to, either.* The smile on Eric's face stopped her from adding that.

"Then, you're in for a treat." He looped the

motorcycle helmets over the handlebars and started pushing the vehicle toward the door in the back of the garage. "Can you get it?"

"Sure." She strode ahead, opened the door, and walked out.

He stopped next to her, flicked the kickstand down, and lifted one of the helmets from the handlebars.

Her heart rate ticked up. She wasn't usually timid about trying new things.

Eric placed one of the helmets on her head and tucked a strand of her hair back from her cheek with a caress that made her heart skitter.

"Uh, no one is here to see us together, so you don't have to pretend."

"Right. Force of habit, I guess." He drew his hand away and walked back to close the garage door.

Amanda had no explanation for herself as to why his moving away left her somewhat bereft.

Eric pulled his helmet on, swung his leg over the motorcycle with masculine grace and kicked up the stand, before turning on the vehicle, balancing it with his firmly planted feet. "Climb on. You can use the foot peg and my arm."

She did as told. His forearm was firm beneath her fingers.

"Now scoot closer and wrap your arms around my waist or you can hold the grips on the sides of the seat."

Amanda chose to wrap her arms around him to which it sounded like he responded, "Good girl." Eric adjusted what she assumed was the throttle and pulled around the shop onto the street at a sedate speed that he increased smoothly to match traffic. After a block, she released the breath she'd been holding and was fully relaxed when he signaled to turn into the parking lot.

She got off and removed her helmet. "That was fun."

"Told you." He pulled the keys for Sonja's car from his front pocket and handed them to her. "Maybe on the ride back to your place, I can detour up the coast highway and you can get the full effect of riding."

Her heart thumped. It was a toss-up whether it was caused by the anticipation of going fast or the thought of having her arms wrapped around him again for a prolonged period.

Eric waited for Amanda to pull out of the parking lot and get a couple blocks ahead of him before he revved the throttle and shot off significantly faster than he'd take off with Amanda. He slowed down once he got on Seaside Boulevard. He caught up with her at the turn to the B&B. They both pulled around to the back of the building.

He gazed over the ocean and the B&B's private beach and an idea took hold. Inviting Amanda to a private evening swim one night. Or was that idea beyond the bounds of public fake romance? She wasn't his usual dalliance, and although he was attracted to her, he valued her friendship too much to mess that up.

His cell phone and the closing of the car door cut short any further thoughts of Amanda in a swimsuit. He checked his text. *Yes!* He would have fist pumped, but if Amanda saw him, she'd wonder why. Even though the romance was a charade, the last thing he wanted was to lie to her, other than the potential lie of omission his text from Liam was about.

"I'll just take the keys in to Sonja, unless you want to come in."

Eric thought about his earlier visit to get the car. Jeff hadn't come by the shop, so chances were good he and the plumber were still working. Or at least Jeff still was. "No, I'll wait out here."

A couple minutes later, Amanda returned with Sonja. "Sonja has to pick up a few things at the store, so she's going to drop me at the city hall for my car. And Mom texted me that she's making fried chicken for your dinner. 6:00 sharp. Don't stand her up."

"You don't want to miss Lisa's fried chicken for anything," Sonja added.

He might. For example, for a private dinner for two with Amanda.

"Okay." He watched the women climb in the car.

"Hey, Eric," Jeff said from the B&B doorway. "Can you give me a hand with something?"

Just what he didn't want to get roped into. "Sure." He walked to the building. He wasn't used to his plans being thrown over so easily. "The plumber didn't solve your problem?"

Jeff led him around the mansion to a half-filled ditch in the front leading to a still-uncovered portion of the B&B's connecting sewer line. "We caught one thing that I didn't know was malfunctioning yet, but the problem with the suite appears to be in the city sewer line."

Eric eyed the two shovels by the ditch.

"The mansion was the first seaside home to have public sewer service, so the lines are old. I've left a message for Public Works."

"I suppose you want me to help you fill in the rest of the ditch."

"And who says action adventure movie actors aren't so bright?"

"No one. You're pushing it."

"We'll be done in time for you to make your dinner. Is Amanda going to be there, too?"

Eric picked up a shovel and shook his head.

"But you'd like her to be." Jeff picked up the other shovel.

"No, I'd rather be somewhere alone with her," Eric said under his breath. Or so Eric had thought.

"That's the way the winds blow, eh?" Jeff dropped a shovel full of dirt in the ditch.

Eric matched him. "You have a problem with that?"

Jeff shook his head. "Not at all."

Eric shoved his shovel into the pile of loose dirt so hard he hit the solid ground beneath it. "Good." He dropped it in the ditch and attacked the pile again.

It was good. He'd established his and Amanda's relationship with someone in town other than Liam at the shop. Not that Jeff would tell anyone else but Sonja. He dropped another shovel-full into the ditch and studied his work. Would Amanda tell Sonja about their deal? Should he tell Jeff?

*Nah.* Not unless his friend heard it elsewhere and asked him.

"Chop, chop. Stop daydreaming about Amanda and get back to work or that fried chicken will be cold by the time you get there," Jeff said.

Eric tightened his grip on the shovel to keep his fingers from giving Jeff the gesture he wanted to.

No, he wouldn't tell him about the charade. But he might ask his friend for advice. For all his prowess at attracting women he wanted and even ones he didn't want, Jeff had a much better track record in keeping a relationship going.

Eric went back to work. He'd been known to screw up one in less time than the time frame for his and Amanda's holiday romance.

# CHAPTER 4

*Today was definitely a TGIF*. Who knew carrying on a fake holiday romance could be so time consuming and tiring? Amanda parked her car next to her beach house, one of the few that hadn't been decorated for Christmas yet. Maybe tomorrow. She grabbed her things and headed up the steps. Her phone pinged.

*Are you sure you don't want to come for dinner? Eric is running late, so you'd have time to get here,* her mother texted.

*Sorry,* she texted back. *I have plans.*

No need to tell Mom that her plans were to microwave the couple leftover slices of pizza in the refrigerator, pour herself a goblet of wine, and sit out on her deck watching the waves.

*All right, then.* Her mother signed off.

Inside, she placed her bag and phone on the

coffee table and went into the kitchen. Eric hadn't said anything about plans for the evening. She'd expected he suggest they do something together later when she'd declined the ride up the coast he'd offered. She'd even come up with a reason she couldn't spend the evening with him, although she'd forgotten it now.

Blaming the hollow feeling in her stomach on hunger, she stuck all the leftover pizza in the microwave and went to change into jeans and a light sweater. Despite the ocean breeze, the evening temperature was holding in the mid-60s. Perfect for sitting out. She debated for two seconds whether to bring her day planner or the new novel she'd picked up earlier in the week out with her. When the microwave dinged, she pulled out the plate and juggled it, along with the goblet, wine bottle, and book, so she'd only have to make one trip.

Amanda placed her feast on the round wooden table and sank into the chair facing the ocean. Its cushions were still warm from the earlier direct sun. Peace and quiet. Nothing but the sound of the waves and a few seagulls. She savored a big bite of pizza. That was one of the reasons she'd bought the cottage when she'd moved to Indigo Bay. The solitude and the challenge of fixing it up herself.

With next to no architectural clients at first, she'd had lot of time on her hands—something she was envious of now. And after years of being rented out, the cottage had needed a total makeover. She leaned back and sipped her wine, closing her eyes to take in just the melodic evening sounds.

Amanda opened her eyes to a young couple, teens, really, walking barefoot in the sand, arms hugged around each other so tightly, she doubted a grain could get between them. They stopped for a lingering kiss. *Ah, young love.* She closed her eyes again to give them privacy. *Any love.* She could hardly remember the last time she'd felt genuinely close to someone she'd dated.

A sound on the wood stairs made her sit up wide-eyed.

"Sorry if I woke you." Eric stood on the top step with a plastic bag in his hand.

"I wasn't dozing, just listening to the sounds. Do you ever do that?" Why did she say that? Amanda took another bite of pizza to occupy her mouth.

"It's not exactly the same, but I like to sit and listen to the fountain behind my house and the birds singing in the trees. It gives me kind of a Zen feeling."

"Yeah. Have a seat."

He sunk into the seat across from her and placed the plastic bag on the table. "But to put things in perspective, I can achieve that same Zen listening to a finely tuned motorcycle or sports car."

She laughed. "Speaking of motorcycles, I didn't hear yours drive up. Or were you in stealth mode."

"You watched another of my early movies."

"I enjoyed it. For what it is," she teased. No need to tell him that since they'd first met, she'd been periodically watching his movies in order and what she'd particularly enjoyed was watching him mature —both as an actor and a man—from a limited-dimension young 20-something to the many-faceted man sitting across from her, staring at her with interest.

She jumped up. "You want some wine? I'll get you a glass."

He looked up at her with a lop-sided smile. "I guess that's a yes, since you're up now and halfway to the door."

She wasn't. Really. She just needed to step away and reorient herself.

"And you might as well take this with you." He handed her the plastic bag. "It's *some* of the leftover fried chicken."

It must have weighed three pounds.

"That's why you didn't hear my bike. I walked to try and burn off some of the chicken I ate. Sonja was right about your mother's fried chicken. I've never had any other close to it." He patted his stomach, drawing her attention to it.

"You don't look any worse the wear for overindulging." Amanda pictured what she imagined from his movies were a well-toned set of abs under the thin fabric of his t-shirt. She truly needed to get herself inside for a moment before she opened her mouth or imagination again.

She escaped inside, put the chicken in the refrigerator, and grabbed another wine goblet before standing still and taking three cleansing breaths. *Better*. Back outside, Eric rested his head against the padded chair back, eyes closed. So still and relaxed, he looked more like he did in the early movies she'd watched than a man closing in on 50.

His eyes opened. She stopped staring and busied herself pouring Eric some wine.

"You know," he started.

His voice startled her, and she sloshed wine over the rim of the glass to the table.

"Let me." Eric took the goblet with one hand and reached for one of the napkins she'd brought out with her pizza. He wiped up the spill. "What I was going to say was that I think you're onto something with your ocean listening. It's relaxing." He eyed his full-to-the-brim wine glass before continuing. "Maybe you should try some more."

Her face heated. *No*, she said to herself as if that could stop her blush. He should be used to women staring at him. Amanda sat, lowered her gaze, and allowed herself a reasonable sip of her wine.

He leaned over and drank enough of his wine to lower the level to where he could pick it up and drink. "You should have come to dinner at your mother's."

"That bad?" she asked, trying to imagine what her mother might have said or done.

"Not really. Let's just say, I now know just about everything about Amanda Jade Strickland from birth to age 18—with pictures."

Amanda palmed her face. She'd thought she was embarrassed before.

"Fortunately …" Eric paused and drank some more wine, his gaze lowering, taking her in, as he placed the empty glass back on the table. "She left the adult Amanda as a Christmas gift for me to unwrap myself."

She squirmed and tried to still the turbulence inside her with a quick, "I don't think you'll find any surprises."

Eric rose, his eyes darkening, "I don't know about that."

She stared, unable to find her voice, and that was before he smiled.

"Thanks for the drink. I'd better get going," he said.

"Um hmm." Her mind was still back on unwrapping.

"Your mother said you might need some help tomorrow with your outside Christmas decorations. I can come by after lunch."

"Sure." She'd never needed help before, but Eric might have said anything, and she would have agreed.

ERIC MENTALLY KICKED himself all the way back to Lisa's place. He hadn't meant to slip into his actor-on-the-move persona with that smarmy unwrap comment. He and Amanda were friends, and he didn't want to jeopardize that friendship. Other than Jeff, he had few real friends. He'd panicked at the way Amanda's embarrassment had made him all protective feeling and lapsed into the cover he wore for most people.

But Amanda wasn't most people. She was someone he could usually be his real self for. And then she'd gotten that dazed look that he normally basked in. From Amanda, it tore at something inside him. As much of an oxymoron as it sounded, he wanted to be as honest with their pretend romance as possible. He'd turn things around with her tomorrow.

# CHAPTER 5

The next morning Eric was at Seaside Cycles before Jeff. He sat in the small back lot waiting for his friend to come and open the shop. The sooner they got his bike tuned and he could clean up, the sooner he could get over to Amanda's cottage and make up for last night. The only way he had thought of to do that was to be truthful and admit that Hollywood sex-symbol Eric Slade was intimidated by women he felt more than a shallow attraction to. Sure he was physically attracted to Amanda. What man wouldn't be. But his attraction went a lot further than that.

Jeff pulled in beside him, shut down his bike, and took off his helmet. "What kind of plot are your hatching?"

"What do you mean?"

His friend swung off his bike and Eric did too. "I know the look."

Eric wavered. "I want an honest relationship with Amanda."

"The only kind worth having." Jeff unlocked, and Eric pushed his bike in.

As he lowered the kickstand, Eric said, "Maya, my last co-star, has been stalking me."

Jeff grabbed a toolbox from a shelf. "Yeah, Sonja and I suspected that. Maya is, what, Chris's age? Not your style."

*Hasn't been for a good while, at least.*

"She was good. You were good together in the movie, though. I didn't see any more in it, except you might be hiding out from her here."

Jeff's words were some relief. But the bigger question was whether his friend also suspected his and Amanda's holiday romance deal. He pushed that thought from his mind. If Jeff did suspect, he'd be all over him about it. They were no-holds-barred friends.

"Kind of, the hiding out part. Now, let's get to work. I have an afternoon appointment with a certain mayor to help her put up her holiday decorations."

Jeff patted him on the back. "I wouldn't want to keep you from that."

With service customers and bike and ATV rentals, his bike tune-up had taken the full morning. He had just enough time to clean up, eat the lunch Lisa had offered to make for him and be at Amanda's by 1:00. Not that he'd given her an exact time. He started to text her that he'd be there in 45 minutes and ask if he should bring any tools, then stopped. He'd told her after lunch. Better to keep it vague, build anticipation.

Eric roared off toward Amanda's cottage. *Yeah, build anticipation.* His at least.

He slowed when he saw an Indigo Bay police car ahead.

Or was it *uncertainty* in his case?

AMANDA FINISHED HER LUNCH DISHES, making it officially after lunch. That was what Eric had said. That he'd help her with the decorations after lunch. So where was he? She glanced over the kitchen bar out the living room's seaside window for the…she'd-lost-count-of-how-many times. After lunch could be anytime from now until the end of the day. She had to stop. She wasn't 100% sure that's what Eric had even said. The second glass of wine must have fogged her mind. The goblets held more than she usually drank.

She pulled the stool from its place by the refrigerator and stepped up to open the ceiling door to the cottage's storage area. Her inside and outside Christmas decorations were about all she had stored there. Her ladder, tools, and other things were in the outside shed.

"Hello," Eric's call through the screen door almost made her drop the door she was holding open with one hand onto her other hand.

She calmed herself and climbed another step to secure the door open. "Hi. Come in." I was getting the decorations."

He let himself in. "I'll do that."

She frowned at him over her shoulder, not quite ready to face him for whatever reason now that he was here.

"I mean, I'm taller." He shrugged.

He looked almost as uncomfortable as she was.

Eric closed the distance to the step stool. "About yesterday evening."

"It was the wine," she blurted. "That's why I was so spacey."

His voice lowered as if he were drawing it from somewhere deep inside. "I want to apologize for being sexist, my sexist unwrap comment, however you want to word it, yesterday."

*Sexy?* She didn't say that aloud, did she? *No laughter*. She must be safe. "Apology accepted." Amanda turned back to her task.

"So, what do you want me to do?"

"I'm already up here, so I'll hand the boxes down to you, once I have them moved to the edge."

"Okay and while I wait, I'll enjoy the view."

A quick glance showed he was still facing her. The heat from the attic combined with her internal temperature. Eric wasn't talking about the ocean view. She resisted fanning herself. Instead, she cleared her throat. Loudly.

"Hey," he teased, standing there in his muscle shirt, despite the fact that it was December, and thigh-hugging faded jeans. "I didn't say I wasn't a man."

That Eric *was* a man was an understatement.

"We men can't help ourselves sometimes."

"Is that right? Well get your manly self over here and help me."

She handed him the boxes with the outdoor lights and garlands, followed by the plastic bag covered wreath for the peak of the cottage. Then, on her toes, Amanda reached with her fingertips for the larger box holding her indoor decorations.

She wobbled with the strain.

"I've got you." Eric gripped her hips firmly.

As if that was going to make her less wobbly. With great forbearance, she inched the box toward the edge where she could grasp it firmly. "I'm good. You can let go any time."

Eric released his grip slowly, weakening her knees and her balance again. They needed to have a talk about touching boundaries as soon as she figured out a way to broach that topic without giving away what his touch was doing to her.

She turned and handed him the box. "That's it."

He took the box, and she scrambled down. When she turned, he'd already deposited the inside decorations box on the floor and picked up both of the outdoor boxes, leaving her just the wreath to carry.

"I can take one of the boxes," she said.

His face became a picture of mock indignation. "What will the neighbors say if they see me letting you carry out big boxes."

She snorted. "Probably what they've said every other year I've carried them out to decorate. Nothing."

"Ah, so seeing me carrying them out may make them talk. That's what we want, isn't it?"

Amanda picked up the wreath. That was what he wanted to quell the rumors about him and his last co-star. She'd been so thrilled about his being here boosting the city celebrations and the animal shelter fundraising that she hadn't thought about her reputation, and position as mayor.

"To be honest, I hadn't thought of that." She followed Eric out.

He looked around as if checking for neighbors or anyone in the vicinity before placing the boxes on the deck. "It shouldn't matter. We're consenting adults, and I don't recall our agreement requiring anything off-base that would stretch the boundaries of our friendship. I mean friends hug and kiss, don't they?" He grinned.

An itch crept down her spine at the thought of Eric's arms around her, lips pressed to hers. "I supposed. It's not like I've never let a guy who I never dated again kiss me goodnight."

His grin retreated some.

"I didn't mean that as a dig," she said. "Small public displays of affection are certainly within our agreement." She'd find a way to control any undue reactions on her part to them as the need arose.

"Okay, then." Eric opened the light box. "Let's get this show going. We're going to need a ladder to get these lights up."

"In the shed," Amanda said, her emotions grounded again.

A while later she stood back and admired their work. It had taken them less than half the time it generally took her to put the lights and the garlands up. All that was left was the wreath, which Eric was working on centering in the triangular peak.

"A little more to the left, a voice behind her called." Lucille and Princess were on the beach, starting for the cottage steps.

"She's right," Amanda confirmed to Eric's back before greeting Lucille. "Nice day for a walk, and for putting up decorations."

"It's warm enough," Lucille agreed. "But the wind is playing havoc with my hair."

Amanda couldn't see that the older woman's hair looked any different than it ever did.

Eric joined them, impressing Lucille if not Amanda by hopping down from several rungs up the ladder.

"Thanks for the help," she said. "Why don't I go in and get us all a drink of sweet tea?"

"I could use a drink." Eric wiped his brow with his hand. "The sun's hot up there."

"I have a few minutes I can spare for a drink." Lucille made herself at home in one of the two chairs.

"If you don't mind, Eric, can you get another deck chair from the shed."

"Sure. I'll put the ladder away, too."

Amanda smiled and nodded her thanks. She returned with a tray with three glasses and a pitcher of tea.

"Sit," Lucille urged. "I have something to tell you before Eric gets back. You know I don't gossip."

Amanda fought not to roll her eyes.

"But I thought you should know. He's seeing someone else."

"Ah, if you mean Maya, that's over." Had never began, according to Eric.

Lucille lowered her voice and shielded her mouth on the side toward the steps he was climbing. "Not Maya. Someone right here in Indigo Bay. I saw it on Facebook. On his fan group page."

"Something interesting on Facebook?" Eric asked.

"Put that chair down and sit, young man." Lucille pointed to the other side of Amanda.

He situated the chair, petted Princess, and sat. It looked like he was in trouble about something.

"I'm going to ask you a question right here in front of Amanda, and I want an honest answer."

"Certainly." He took the glass of tea Amanda had for him and avoided eye contact with her so he could keep his amusement out of his expression.

"Are you toying with our Amanda's affections?"

Amanda made a choking sound, and he almost lost it. "What do you mean?"

Lucille fanned her hand toward the decorations ending with him and Amanda. "I keep running into you two together, and here you are again." She paused dramatically. "But your Facebook fan page shows you right here in Indigo Bay at Seaside Cycles with an unidentified woman on the back of your motorcycle." Lucille crossed her arms and Precious barked in agreement.

Amanda laughed. A false laugh if he was hearing right, and he might be getting older and falling apart in other ways, but his hearing was fine.

"That was me," Amanda said.

"Yesterday at Seaside Cycles?" Lucille asked. "You're sure?"

"I'm sure."

"Good. I'm relieved. Now, Princess and I need to finish our walk."

Eric waited until Lucille was out of hearing distance. "And spread the news about us being a couple."

"About that," Amanda said. "What do you know about the Facebook post about us?"

"I haven't seen it." That was the truth. He hadn't. Eric raised his glass of tea so her gaze couldn't meet his.

"Not my question."

Eric tried not to squirm in his seat. He had vowed to be honest with her in their deal. "Liam might have taken a picture of us at Jeff's shop, and he might have sent it to the president of my national fan club."

"And why might Liam have done that?"

He was in trouble. He couldn't read the twitch in her lips. "Because I asked him to?"

"We have to add another provision to our deal. No more stunts like that."

"I'm sorry."

"I hope so. I have my reputation and position here to protect. We're a little more conservative here about those things than you might be."

"I understand." He dropped his chin. "What's the provision you want to add to our agreement?"

"That neither of us releases any publicity without the consent of the other."

"Agreed. I can be impulsive at times. Friends again?"

Amanda cocked her head with a wry smile. "Friends again."

His heart warmed. And maybe more if he played his role right and honestly.

"With that out of the way, can you give me a couple publicity shots? I told Violet Montgomery, who's heading up the fundraising committee thatI'd get her some. We want to play up your bit at the shelter adoption day."

"Sure." He knew just the ones he'd send.

"Great." She paused. "There's something more."

"Okay." What else had he done?

"How are you and my mother getting on?"

"Good, as far as I can tell."

"How much is she fussing over and taking care of you?"

"That's hard to say."

"More than Sonja would at the B&B?"

"Definitely, but Jeff is always after Sonja not to do anything special for me."

Amanda placed her palms flat on the table. "This may help. You know how I said she'd spent the last five years taking care of my ill father who she hadn't seen for years? She literally did hardly anything but that." Amanda mouth twisted in distaste. "Mom's definition of true love. I think she just didn't know what she'd do with herself once she retired out of the Army."

"I see." He did and he didn't. Jeff had devoted much of his time taking care of his first wife when she was dying of cancer. That had been out of love. But they'd been married more than 20 years and working partners in his custom bike shop in California. "What would you like me to do?"

"Discourage her from doting on you too much. You judge what's too much. Encourage her to get out. Take her out. Have her show you some of the local sights."

He'd planned to do that with Amanda. "So you're asking me if I can juggle two ladies at the same time. No sweat. But what will Lucille and the other townspeople say?" He grinned.

Amanda laughed and batted him playfully.

He caught her hand and an unreadable to him sober expression crossed her sun-kissed face.

"Did you think of a problem?" he asked.

"No, no. Not at all."

If that was the truth, why was his gut telling him otherwise?

Or was that his ego wanting it to be jealousy?

# CHAPTER 6

Amanda hadn't noticed before how much of a chameleon Eric could be, which didn't make him the easiest person to be with for extended periods. Their friendship had been long-distance for the most part, with her seeing him once or twice whenever he came to Indigo Bay to visit Jeff and Sonja. Friday night and Saturday while they were decorating the cottage, he'd slipped back and forth between Eric Slade film star and Eric, Jeff's—and her—friend. She preferred the friend version. So when he'd texted her yesterday that her mother had some work for him to do on her house, Amanda had been relieved rather than disappointed.

But then, he hadn't texted or called last night. She lifted the dress she'd picked out for work today and dropped it back on her bed, realizing she'd chosen it because she knew she looked nice in it. She generally dressed in business casual for work unless something important was on her schedule. Eric wasn't business-important. Besides, she had no idea whether she'd be seeing him today. Amanda put the dress back and took out a just-above-the-knee-length skirt with a cute matching short-sleeved jacket top.

"Good morning," A few minutes later, Eric's voice filled the car when she tapped her dashboard screen to answer his call.

"And good morning to you."

"Do we have any plans for tonight?"

"No. Is this a come-on to an invitation?"

"Very astute, Ms. Mayor," he teased. "Lucille has invited us to dine with her and Princess."

Amanda's stomach sank. "I can't. The planning committee is meeting this evening."

"Do you have to go?"

"I don't have to, but I should. Can we reschedule?" She surprised herself at how easily she thought of them as a couple.

"If you don't mind, I have another idea. Two, in fact."

Amanda slowed to pull into the city hall parking lot. "I'm listening."

"Why don't I take your mother. You said she needs to socialize more."

She *had* said that. So why didn't it sound like a good idea now? She shut off her car. "Sure. What's your other idea?"

Amanda could picture him leaning back in a chair on her mother's porch or the recliner in the other room as she'd noticed he did when he voiced an idea including the two of them.

"If Sonja and Jeff get the problem with the suite at the B&B fixed and can rent it to someone else for the time I reserved, I thought I'd stay here. There's a lot of work that could be done on the house to keep me busy. And I think it's doing your mother good. She seems looser already. That tightness around her lips she had when we met is gone."

Eric would notice that? She yanked the door handle. Of course he would. He was an actor and director. He'd be more attuned to expressions than the average person.

"I don't know."

"Without that pinched look, she looks ten years younger."

Amanda stopped dead, halfway across the parking lot. Ten years younger. She did the math. Mom was closer in age to Eric than she was. Only by months, but still. "You don't think people might talk?" When she took care of herself, Mom was a very attractive woman who'd always looked younger than her age. They'd been mistaken as sisters on numerous occasions.

He laughed, which her instincts didn't know whether to take as good or bad.

"Obviously, you don't read the tabloids. I always

date younger women. At times, significantly younger."

Amanda strode across the rest of the parking lot to the city hall entrance. *Like her.*

"Unless you're jealous," he shot, filling in her silence.

"Of course not." She had been for a second, but that was ridiculous from all corners. "I have friends of all ages."

"Right," he drawled. "Our romance is pretend. How could you be jealous?"

She went inside. Had her *friends* comment stung like his pretend one had? Her phone beeped a call from the public works department. "I have to take this. Go ahead and talk with Sonja and Mom about your accommodations." As if he needed her permission.

"Okay. Bye."

"Hello," she took her work call and headed to her office.

"Amanda, we have a problem," the head of public works said. She entered her office and sat down at her desk as he continued. "The problem at the Mansion B&B is a broken sewage line. It also affects the public beach facilities and the few structures in between. Fortunately, since it's the off-season, they haven't had any backup. Yet."

"I see. Can't the line be repaired?" She wasn't sure why he was calling.

"Not well. It needs to be replaced like we did with the line for the board walk and the rest of the boulevard last spring."

She didn't have to wait for what she knew he was going to say next. "And you don't have enough department money to do that until the first of next year."

"Exactly."

"There's a planning committee meeting this evening wrapping up the planning for the holiday events. I'll expand it to the city council, and you should be there if you weren't already planning to attend."

"Copy that."

"And close the public beach facilities and notify everyone who may be effected by the shutdown and repairs."

"On it. And I'll send you an estimate of repairs for the meeting."

"Yes." She should have thought of that. "As soon as you can. I'll have to see where we can propose to move money from. Keep me updated if there's anything else I need to know before the meeting. Bye."

Amanda stared at her desktop. Like many small cities and towns that operated on a calendar year, Indigo Bay budgeted closely, and most departments depleted or nearly depleted their funds by December. There was the small reserve fund. Highway might have some to spare. And there was the charitable matching contribution she'd talked the city council members into okaying from their municipal salaries for the animal shelter campaign. She pressed her lips together. Not all of the council members liked the idea, but they'd finally all agreed. Some might be more willing to defer some of their pay to public works.

Elbows on the desk, she dropped her head into her hands. Just what she didn't need when she was trying to host the best holiday season ever in Indigo Bay. She lifted her head and sighed before picking up her cell phone which had all the council members' numbers. She went to her contacts and pressed what she thought was her contact icon for Dallas Harper, one if the council members. It went directly to voicemail.

"Hi, you've reached 888-228-5966."

*Eric's number.* She slammed *end call,* her heart pounding. She must not have been looking closely. Or she was falling into a habit of bouncing things off Eric and automatically called his number.

A habit she needed to break right now. Memories of her disastrous graduate school relationship flashed through her mind. Before habit became dependence.

Lucille and her little rat dog were a hoot. But there was only so much he could take of dining and conversation with the two older women, so Eric was glad to drive Lisa home with her car and take a ride along the coast highway on his bike to clear his head. On his way back, he noticed lights still on at the city hall. He cruised into the parking lot to see Amanda's car still there. Her meeting must not be over.

Or maybe it was. As he circled the bike back around to leave, the parking lot door opened, and a couple groups of people walked out. No one he recognized. He pulled his bike up next to Amanda's SUV, shut the motor down, and lowered the kickstand.

"Hey, Eric," one of the women called when he removed his helmet.

"Hey, Lauren," he called back, watching Jeff's daughter-in-law leave the group she was with and walk over.

"I didn't recognize you at first, but I'd know one of my father-in-law's bikes anywhere."

"Jeff can't take all the credit for this one. We rebuilt it together in the old days. What brings you out?" He nodded toward city hall.

"My law practice is on retainer to the city, so I was at the council and planning board meetings."

"How about you?"

"Oh, I'm here picking up chicks."

Lauren laughed. "One in particular, I'm guessing."

He assumed one of his innocent poses.

"Here she comes now. I'll leave you to your pickup. I'm sure I'll see you again before you head back to California. Maybe dinner with Jesse, Shelley, and me. Chris, too, if he's still meeting you here for Christmas."

"Sounds good."

"Hi." Amanda approached him. "Let me guess. You're here hitting on women, and Lauren turned you down."

Had she overheard him or was he that much of a stereotype? He placed his hand over his heart. "I'm wounded. I don't hit on married women or anyone under 35."

"Whew!" she said. "I made the cut."

"With years to spare."

A funny look passed over her face. Or it could have been the shadows. "Long day."

"Yes, made longer by a group of people who have difficulty coming to a consensus."

"How about a nightcap?"

"I could use one."

He pulled his helmet on visor up. "I'll follow you to your place to drop off your car and then, we can go…where?"

"We can stay at the cottage." She clicked her key fob and opened the SUV.

"No, I want to take you out. Show you off."

"I'm not young enough to be a trophy. So what am I? An arm ornament?"

"Not even close. You're a precious gem." He wasn't entirely kidding. Amanda was a gem. The only real gem he'd ever gotten this close to.

Amanda laughed and shook her head. "I'll see you at the cottage."

Eric gave her a head start, so he wouldn't be tailgating her and could center himself and not get stupid while they were out.

Even with the head start, he'd caught up with her by the time she'd reached her driveway. When he turned off the bike, she called to him, "I'm going to run in and change out of my skirt."

"Need any help?"

"And here I thought you were a gentleman," she shot back in a thick Carolina accent.

"I'll confess to the man part."

She waved him down. "Cool your engines." Amanda looked at the bike before pinning his gaze. "Both of them. I'll be right out."

Minutes later, she appeared on the deck. If she was serious about him keeping his engine cool, what she'd changed into didn't encourage that. Skinny jeans and a light sweater that softly skimmed her curves. She had a jacket over one arm.

"Do you think I'll be okay without my jacket for the ride?"

"Yeah." Once she had her arms wrapped around him, he'd be warm enough for both of them. "Hop on. Where are we going?"

"Sweet Caroline's Café should still be open." Amanda put on the helmet that had been fastened to the back of the seat.

"It sells drinks?" He waited for her to flip up the face shield to talk.

"It does if you want coffee or tea. I know. Probably not what you were thinking. But tomorrow is a workday for me. And some of the people from the meeting were headed over."

Eric kept his frown to himself. "I thought you were clocked off work for the day."

"I am. This is more about me showing you off as *my* arm ornament. Get people talking and posting. Send Maya the message that you're taken. Better than that blurry photo on Facebook of the back of my head in a helmet."

He nodded and put his face shield down. He wasn't sure where he stood on being her arm ornament, but he liked the idea of him being taken by her.

WITH HER ARMS tight around Eric's waist, Amanda didn't think about anything but him, the hum of the bike and the cool wind on her back for the short ride to Caroline's. When he stopped in front of the café, and she swung her leg off the bike, uncertainty set in. She glanced in the front window and spied numerous people she knew. She and Eric should have stuck to his plan and gone to some out-of-the-way place for a drink, preferably not in Indigo Bay.

"Need some help?"

Before she could answer, Eric had stepped close and was unfastening her helmet strap. In the process, he ran his forefinger along her jaw line as he removed the strap. She would have given into the impulse to grab his forearms to steady her knees, but for the suspicion that he had caressed her for effect. She was going to have to speak with him about their acting borders.

"I had it." She lifted off the helmet and cradled it in her right arm.

Eric did the same, holding his in his left hand. Was he left-handed? She hadn't noticed.

He slipped his hand in hers, weaving his fingers though her fingers. "We need to make us look real. Holding hands is something a couple moving from friendship to something more would do."

"Thank you, Mr. Director."

"Although in one of my movies, we might be …"

She elbowed him. "Only in your dreams."

An odd expression crossed his face before he let go of her hand to open the door for her.

"Hey, Caroline, you still open?" Eric called to the

owner, a fifty-ish woman who was a mainstay of Indigo Bay's tourist business.

"I was closing when there seemed to be a run on coffee and cinnamon buns, which I'll take since it's off-season. I have three buns left from this morning."

"We'll take them and …" He motioned to Amanda as if he'd just remember her.

"A medium dark roast if you have any left. With creamer."

Caroline smiled and nodded before looking back at Eric.

"The same, large, black," he said.

"I'll freshen the buns in the microwave and bring your order over," Caroline said.

"Thanks." Eric moved closer to Amanda and placed his hand on the small of her back.

She resisted the impulse to move away for two reasons. One, as he'd reminded her, they were supposed to be acting like a couple and two, she liked it.

"Two seats here," Caroline's son Dallas said as he moved down a chair to give them seats next to each other at the family-size table the group from the city hall meeting were gathered at.

Amanda glanced over at her colleagues. It looked like her and Eric's charade was working and that none of her friends appeared the least surprised.

Eric pulled out a chair for her before she could do it herself. She sat. "I guess I didn't get the invitation," she said unable to swallow the small hurt that no one had said anything about going to Caroline's after the meeting.

"We'd thought you had a better offer," Dallas said, nodding at Eric.

Only Eric's preening at the other man's words stopped her from blushing. She tapped his foot under the table, and he stopped.

Caroline brought their coffee and buns over. At the delicious smell of the warmed buns, Amanda's stomach growled. "Excuse me, she said. "I got caught up on a project at work and didn't get to grab anything to eat before the meeting."

"You'd better take the plate with two buns," Eric said, sliding it in front of her as she took her coffee from Caroline.

"We can split the third one," she said.

"No, as one-of-a-kind delicious as Caroline's cinnamon buns are, I can make the sacrifice." He paused before adding a dramatic, "For you."

"Maybe, I'd better take all three," she said. "I think you're syrupy sweet enough."

"Not a chance." He lifted the bun on the plate in front of him and took a big bite.

Amanda busied her mouth with a large swig of coffee.

The group talked about the holiday festivities and the animal shelter's fundraiser, carefully avoiding some of the contentious points of each that they'd hammered out at the meeting. Gradually, they all finished their drinks and exited, leaving just them and Caroline.

"We should let Caroline close. I can take the rest of my cinnamon bun with me."

"Right." He finished his coffee. "I just need the, uh, facilities, and then I'll settle up."

Amanda couldn't help but find Eric's discomfort at saying he had to use the bathroom endearing.

Eric was hardly out of his seat before Caroline came over. "So you and our visiting celebrity?"

"Um. We're trying it out."

"Good for you. And don't worry, you won't hear any gossip about it from me."

"I'm not worried. Now, some of my opposition colleagues could be another story."

Caroline laughed.

"So, what do I owe?" Eric asked, returning and walking her and Caroline to the counter.

"It's on the house." Caroline winked at Amanda.

"You didn't pay, did you?" He asked as they stepped outside.

Amanda halted with feigned affront. "What and diminish your man-of-action mystique in Caroline's eyes? Never."

"That's certainly a relief."

"Almost as much as having that group tet-a-tet with my fellow guardians of the city over."

"I thought it went well." He put his free arm around her waist and pulled her to his side.

"No one's around, we can cut the act."

Eric nuzzled her ear, alerting her nerves twice as much and the coffee had, and kissed her cheek.

"What act?"

# CHAPTER 7

Fueled by the fact that Amanda had been silent in voice and action about his display of affection, Eric woke up the next day more rested than he'd felt in a good long time. Knowing when not to push his luck, he'd dropped her off at her place, not even turning his bike off, although he waited until she was safely inside before roaring off. He couldn't resist that.

"Good morning," he said to Lisa, who appeared to be going out when he came down.

"Good morning. I'm going grocery shopping. Anything particular you want?"

"Yes." He reached in his wallet and pulled out two hundred-dollar bills.

Lisa stiffened, taking on the pinched look she'd had when he'd first met her. "You're already paying for your room and board with the house repairs."

He kept the money out. "That was before I told you that it looks like I'll be here more than a couple days."

"You didn't tell me that."

"I am now." He shot her a practiced winsome smile. "Amanda told me last night that the whole sewer line from the Mansion B&B to the public beach has to be replaced before the suite can be rentable."

"Oh. Poor Sonja and Jeff. What about the rest of the B&B? What about the ballroom? The gala there?"

"Oddly, the suite and is on a separate outflow line with the unoccupied caretaker's house, which was added after the mansion was built."

"That's good for Sonja and the gala. I still don't need your money, though. I've always taken care of myself."

And others, from what Amanda had told him. He put the bills back. "Okay, for now." He'd figure out another way to repay her.

Lisa's face softened. "Did you and Amanda have a nice time last night?"

She caught him off-guard. Nothing like jumping topics. "What do you mean?"

Lisa shrugged. "Facebook. I saw a picture of the group of you at Caroline's."

"Oh, yeah. We did." He made a mental note to let Amanda know he'd had nothing to do with that post.

"Good." Her face took on an earnest expression, he'd seen Amanda's on occasion. "I don't need to know if this is just a holiday fling or what. Amanda needs some fun in her life. If you can give her that fun, more power to you."

Eric swallowed the elation that welled at Lisa's apparent approval.

"But one important thing."

The elation evaporated.

"Be upfront with her. She's been hurt in the past."

"I will." He'd already crossed that line and been read the riot act.

"So what do you have planned for today?" she asked as she picked up her purse.

"Since it's cool this morning, I'm going to check out those missing roof shingles. See if any more are loose."

"You're okay with no one here. I mean if you slip …"

"I'll be careful."

"Then, see you later." Lisa left.

His first inclination was to check his Facebook profile. He stopped. He didn't have a presence there, rarely checked it, and wasn't friends with anyone he knew in Indigo or anywhere else. But he could have fan club members here who were friends or family of whoever had posted the picture at Caroline's that Lisa had seen. He closed his eyes trying to remember if he'd seen anyone with their phones out last night. He had, but the phones had been sitting on the table.

Might as well check the damage. He pulled his

own phone from his pocket and went to his fan page. There it was. Taken through the window of the café. With the written post: Mystery woman identified. It wasn't a bad picture of the two of them talking with Caroline. It had been posted by one of the fan page administrators, so he didn't know who had taken the picture and sent it to the page. He should have asked Lisa how she'd seen it. He was sure she didn't frequent his fan page.

Eric weighed whether this required a city hall appearance, which he certainly wouldn't mind making. But he did want to get any roof repairs made before the heat of the day. He texted Amanda.

*We made my fan page again. Not my doing.*

*I know and I know. Mom alerted me that she'd seen it, thanks to Lucille.*

Lucille was on Facebook? He shook his head. And probably every other social media platform.

*You think she took the picture?*

*No. She probably shared it. Want me to check Lucille's profile. We're friends.*

*Nah, I don't really need to know as long as you're okay with it.*

*I am.*

Amanda didn't sound thrilled about it. Eric thought about Lisa's warning.

*It may end up in a tabloid.*

*I accept that comes with the territory.*

*Okay. Talk to you later?*

Leaving that as a question would open it to Amanda contacting him. He didn't want to be the only one pursuing their relationship. And, despite it being behind him suggesting the fake romance, he needed to think about exposing them to what she'd said comes with the territory.

That and his suddenly growing aversion to the spotlight he'd put them in.

"You have a call from a Chris Slade," Tracy said when Amanda picked up her office phone. "Do you want to take it?"

Why would Eric's son be calling her? She'd only met him once, when he came to Indigo Bay just after he'd gotten out of the service. "Yeah, I'll take it."

Tracy clicked the call through.

"Hi, Chris."

"Mayor Strickland."

"Yes." The voice didn't sound like Chris, but she'd never talked to him on the phone before."

"This is Graham Backland. From *Scoop* …"

One of the tackiest of the tabloid magazines. "No comment." Amanda hung up and buzzed Tracy. "If you got a caller ID number on that call, put it on our don't accept calls list."

"I'm sorry. That wasn't Chris Slade? The ID said

Private Caller. I thought with him being Eric's son and all, he was protecting his phone number."

"No, it was one of the tabloid magazines."

"What did they want?"

"I didn't ask. Put any call for me from unknown numbers or private callers directly through to my voicemail."

"All right."

Amanda tried to get her concentration back on the list of raffle gifts and silent auction items for the gala received so far from local businesses and residents. She wanted to give Sonja an idea of what would be dropped off at the B&B ahead of the event and project a ballpark amount the animal shelter might receive.

But the only projection her mind was forming was not enough. Items or gala tickets. Despite the excellent promotion Gina Andrews had done getting signs about the gala and other fundraising activities up all over town. Too bad it wasn't blazing across social media the way her and Eric's charade was. *That was it.*

She punched in Eric's number, and her call went directly to his voicemail. He may have gotten the same call she did. Or he could be busy with work for her mother or at Seaside Cycles with Jeff. He didn't say earlier what he had on tap for today. Not that she expected him to report into her daily. Well, she kind of did, but only if he wanted to.

Amanda decided to move the data she had on the list on her desk to Excel to help with her projections. Once she had her spreadsheet created and started adding the information, her mind wandered to last night … what he said about not pretending.

Her office phone rang. She weighed whether to let it go to voicemail. Amanda picked it up. Tracy would have fielded any calls that weren't dialed directly to her number.

"Hello. Mayor Strickland," she said.

"Good morning mayor," Eric said. "You called?"

Was there a slight huskiness in his voice? No, more likely in her brain affecting its functions. "Yes, I did, with official business."

"City business or our deal business?"

"A little of both," she said after a moment of disappointment that he seemed to see them both on the same plain.

"Ah, let me hear it."

Amanda explained her concerns about the fundraising and gala ticket sales. "My thought is to get a feature in the happenings section of the Charleston daily newspaper stressing your participation in both. We don't have a lot of time to pull it off."

"And it would help if I had my publicity people be the contact."

"Exactly."

"Where do you want the interview? I assume you want an interview."

"That's the goal. I'm going back and forth about the location. The B&B since the gala is there or the shelter for the emotional impact."

"Let's leave it up to my people. Maybe they can get coverage of the gala, too."

"Great. Get back to me as soon as you know anything."

"I will. Or sooner. How about supper at your mother's tonight and a stroll along Seaside Boulevard and the beach afterwards to look at the holiday decorations."

"Another photo opportunity like us at Caroline's?"

"No." He still sounded confused. "I thought you might like to."

"I would. Definitely. I'll change and come over right after I finish my afternoon work."

"See you then."

Amanda held the phone receiver in her hand for a few moments after Eric had hung up. Had her mother said something to him about her love of seeing everything decorated for the holidays?

She placed the receiver firmly on the phone. No. She preferred to think that Eric knew her well enough to come up with the idea himself.

To please her.

ERIC GOT RIGHT on contacting his promotion team, who jumped on it being good publicity for him, although he stressed it was for the animal shelter.

"I see the interview as being with both you and the Indigo Bay mayor. At the shelter. Definitely at the shelter with pictures of you with the animals," his publicist said.

"I'm not sure that's what the mayor wants."

"No, you need that. Let me send you a link to what's in the *Scoop* blog today. It makes your friend the mayor sound about as appealing as a root canal."

Eric's hackles rose, even before he clicked the link to the blog. There was that picture taken at Seaside Cycles, followed by what looked to be Amanda's official biography pasted from the Indigo Bay website with snide and derogatory comments from the blog writer interspersed throughout. He bit back the words that came to his tongue. The blog ended with, *How far has America's formerly most sought-after star fallen?* followed by a terse *Ms. Strickland declined to comment.* Eric's bitten-back words came out in a torrent.

His agent sighed. "Now that that's out of your system, you see why your friend needs to be included in the interview."

"Yeah and why the blog writer needs to be

blasted off the top of a skyscraper," Eric said, referring to a scene in one of his movies.

"Hold off on that, and we'll set up the newspaper gig."

"Thanks, and can you express print copies of a couple of my publicity photos. Amanda, the mayor, wants them for publicity here. I have electronic copies, but print is better."

"You'll have them tomorrow. To your friend's B&B? Anything else?

"That would be good and no." Eric clicked off and punched Amanda office number. "It's me. Call when you have a chance."

He checked the shingles while he waited for a callback from Amanda before grabbing his helmet from the house and heading back out to his bike. She must be busy. Eric put his helmet on and fastened the chin strap. He couldn't expect her to drop everything and take his call whenever he phoned. She had a life. Another life, he corrected himself, besides the one he was beginning to think they had together. Smiling, he swung onto his bike, cruised to the local hardware store to order the paint Lisa had decided on to be delivered to the house, and headed back to finish the new front porch railing he'd started yesterday.

Lisa returned home as he was nailing down the last piece of the top rail. "Looking good," she said.

"You, too," he returned, taking in the rich brown

with honey highlights that had replaced her salt and pepper hair color.

"Thank you." She smiled as she walked up the steps. Amanda has been after me forever to do something. In a nice way."

"Speaking of Amanda." Eric started putting the tools Jeff had lent him in Jeff's toolbox. "Hope you don't mind that I invited her to eat with us this evening."

"Mind? Not at all. I'd have her join us every night."

Eric laughed. "I thought we'd make it a joint effort. If I can borrow your car, I'll pick up some steaks and get the propane tank for your grill filled so I can grill them. You can do the sides?"

"Fine with me." She opened the screen door.

"Ah." Eric shuffled his feet. "Before you go in, I want to ask something else about Amanda."

Lisa grinned. Most likely at the school-boy uncertainty that had invaded his body. The first grin he'd ever seen from her.

"I thought I'd take her on a walk to look at the Christmas decorations around town," he said double checking his plans even though Amanda had agreed.

"She'll like that. Christmas is her favorite holiday. She can't get enough of the decorations, everything to do with the season. She's probably told you I was an Army nurse."

He nodded.

"Christmas was the one holiday I could usually count on having off to spend with her. So, we did things up big. For her, there can't be too much Christmas."

"Good to know."

"It's so magical, she's even willing to accept surprises at Christmastime. I'm sure you know how she is with her planning. She leaves no room for surprises."

He thought about her reaction to the unexpected publicity about them and about her surprise pickup at the Charleston airport. Except for surprising others? Maybe only certain others. His heart thrummed. Like him?

"So," Lisa continued. "At Christmas she's open to surprises, good surprises, that don't disrupt her plans too much."

Eric processed that information and laughed. "I think I have that. Don't be late for Christmas dinner unless I have a just-what-she-always-wanted-gift with me."

Lisa laughed back. "Breaking it down to its essence, yes. And, um…" Now it was her turn to hesitate. "You and whatever you have going with my daughter. I think it's good for her."

Lisa left him with that. What he heard as expectations. Of him. His chest tightened.

And aside from acting, he had a losing record of fulfilling other people's expectations.

# CHAPTER 8

Amanda breezed into her architecture office. She had a couple hours of simple work, and she'd be done for the day. Done and able to leave in plenty of time to get home, change, and be ready for supper at Mom's. And for strolling with Eric under the stars, enjoying the unusually warm weather they were having today.

She turned on her computer, clicked her design program to complete her proposal drawing and nothing happened. She'd clicked again, then shut down and tried once more. Amanda huffed. She had no idea what the problem was. All her software was up to date. She regularly ran spyware and antivirus programs and did routine computer maintenance. "There shouldn't be a problem," she told the computer.

Amanda tried a recovery program she hadn't ever

had to use before. She slapped the desk when that did nothing. Finally, she gave in and unloaded and reloaded the program. The reload did the trick. She checked the computer clock and saw she'd lost an hour's work time. She worked as quickly as she could without sacrificing quality to finish. The printer cranked out the drawings at what felt like a snail's pace. She had to get to the post office. If she wanted to clinch the job—and she did—the drawings had to be in the prospective client's hands tomorrow morning.

A power walk later, she left the Post Office. Drawings sent Priority Mail. Mission accomplished. She'd need to keep up that pace if she wanted to be at Mom's by six, since she hadn't driven to work today and had to walk to the cottage.

Her cell phone, punctuated by a clap of thunder, interrupted her start. After this morning's call, the private caller on the caller ID discouraged her from answering. She waited on the Post Office steps a minute for the voicemail message she'd get if the call had been anyone she knew. A minute too long. The increasingly dark clouds released a deluge.

Great. It was a toss-up which was closer, her office or her mother's house. Or she could wait here, back pressed to the Post Office wall, taking advantage of the slight overhang to try to keep dry and maybe wait out the rain. The sky to the east looked a little brighter already.

A car horn honked across the street. Her mother's car with Eric at the wheel. She took a deep breath and released it. So much for her plans to dress for their after-supper stroll. She waved. Eric did a U-turn and pulled to the curb in front of the Post Office.

He rolled down the passenger side window. "Stay there." He got out of the car and fiddled with something before standing upright under a pink polka dotted umbrella.

Amanda tried, really tried not to laugh. But it was a lost cause. "Nice umbrella," she said.

"Is that any way to treat your rescuer?" He assumed a pout that was as incongruous as the umbrella.

"I thank you, kind sir." She stepped out from the wall and under the umbrella. "How did you know I was at the Post Office?"

"I didn't. When it started clouding up, your mother suggested I drive by your office and the city hall to check for your car, since you might have walked to work. No car either place, and the lights were out at your office. I was on my way back to your mother's place."

A shot of disappointment pierced her that his mission had been her mother's idea and not his. "You could have called."

He opened the car door for her, and she ducked in. "The Private Caller." She pushed a strand of hair that had escaped her French twist back from her face. "You didn't leave a message."

"My bad," he said before jogging around to the other side of the car and climbing in. "I figured you'd see my number and call back. I forgot I had Private Caller on to make a couple calls about building materials."

"I guess I forgive you. A downside of dating a movie star."

"So, tonight's an official date?"

"You asked me to dinner and a stroll around town. Yep a date."

He flicked on the directional to pull out. "Your place or your mother's?"

Amanda checked the dashboard clock. It was close to 6:00, the family supper time, and her mother was a stickler for being on time. "Mom's. I'm not really wet, except for my hair, which I can dry there," she said as he pulled another U-turn. "Watch it, you're going to get yourself in trouble with Indigo Bay's finest."

"And the mayor?"

"Maybe."

"Promises, promises. But I thought women liked bad boys."

She never had. Until now.

He patted her knee and she almost jumped from the jolt. "Especially good women."

*Good women.* For whatever reason his quip the

other night about not hitting on married women sounded in Amanda's head. Her playful mood dimmed. She wasn't as goody-goody as Eric thought. But their relationship was pretend. She glanced at his craggy profile and his pure maleness took her breath away. Except it was becoming less and less pretend. At least on her part.

She looked out the side window at the sun returning from behind the rain clouds. She'd tell him tonight. Even if it ruined the date. Amanda blinked at the brightness of the evening sun.

Even if it put a halt to what was growing between them.

AMANDA WAS UNUSUALLY quiet on the drive home. He wracked his brain for something he might have inadvertently said. And came up with nothing. Her subdued manner became more pronounced after she took Lisa up on her offer to use her hairdryer and joined them at the dining room table. He was no psychologist, but he sensed that Amanda and Lisa shared a strong mother-daughter love, but there was some hidden line drawn between them.

But he told himself that it wasn't any of his business and went about regaling both women over the supper table with Hollywood and movie stories, along with a couple about him and Jeff as teens.

"Anyone have room for dessert?" Lisa asked when they finished. "I have raspberry pie from Caroline's and hand-churned vanilla ice cream."

"Mom, you should have said something before I had that second helping of your potato salad," Amanda said with the most pep she'd shown since they'd arrived.

"Tell you what. Why don't you and Eric start your stroll with the boardwalk and beach and finish with Seaside Boulevard. Then you can come back and have dessert if you want."

"Great idea," Eric said.

Amanda agreed. "And can I borrow some better walking shoes? My sandals are comfortable but won't be once they're filled with sand." She rose and began clearing the table.

"Tennis shoes or slip-ons?" her mother asked.

"Tennis shoes."

Lisa nodded. "I'll be right back."

He stood and picked up his plate and flatware.

"You don't have to. I've got this, and you're already doing so much around here."

"Hey, I'd be doing it if I were at Jeff and Sonja's." He followed her into the kitchen.

Lisa was back when they returned to the dining room. "I'll take care of the rest." She handed her shoes to Amanda. "You two get off on your date."

Amanda stiffened. Or it looked to him like she had. But the stroll technically was a date, even if it was a pretend date. His cell phone buzzed. He pulled it out and glanced at it. "I should take this." He left the women alone and stepped into the living room.

Both were smiling when he stepped back into the dining room, and he had news that should keep that smile on Amanda's face. "That was my PR manager. She got us an interview with the Charleston paper."

Amanda jumped up, eyes bright. "Yes!"

Eric's heart warmed. He knew the excitement was for the interview and what it could do for the animal shelter benefit, but he and his people could take credit for making it happen.

"When?"

"Thursday for the Wednesday before the gala. It's the best she could do. The paper is having a holiday-doings feature page that day. And we'll have to do it at the newspaper office."

"That's not perfect. But still may attract some people to the gala and, definitely, people to the shelter tours." She pulled out her cell phone. "I have to tell …"

He stepped to her side and put his hand over hers on the phone. "Work is over."

She tensed again. This time he felt it in her hand and in his stomach.

"You're right." She slipped her hand from under his and put her phone away. "We're supposed to be viewing the holiday decorations around town."

Despite her words, he couldn't say that she was

any more relaxed or that she wasn't looking at their stroll as part of her job.

"Ready," she asked after she had the tennis shoes tied.

Physically, yes, after all the food he'd eaten. Emotionally, he had no idea. "Let's go."

Once outside, he took her hand, and she didn't object. She didn't say anything.

"Did I say or do something in the car?" he blurted when they reached the corner of Seaside Boulevard to cross over to the boardwalk and the beach. "You're so quiet."

"I'm enjoying the quiet. Being with you."

He'd take that as a positive.

"You did say something. In the car."

Supper churned in his stomach as he tried to second guess what he might have said that bothered her.

She stopped when they hit the boardwalk and looked up at him under the holly-wrapped streetlight. He was so tempted to dip down and kiss her before she could speak.

"Can I ask you something?"

Too late. He straightened. "Anything."

"It's none of my business, but did you cheat on your wives?"

Eric started. That came out of nowhere. "I did not. Nor do I date married, or otherwise taken women."

Stricken was the only word for Amanda's

expression. "No, please don't tell me you're secretly engaged," he pleaded with exaggerated humor. He knew she wasn't. Jeff or Sonja would have warned him off. Unless… he choked for breath. Unless it was truly secret.

"Of course not. I wouldn't do that to you."

"I didn't think so." His assurance didn't bring any color back to her face.

"But I was once." Her voice was barely above a whisper. "Secretly engaged to a married man."

"The bad relationship when you were in grad school." He pulled her into his arms. "I don't need to know."

"Yes, you do," her muffled voice said against his chest. "What I'm beginning to feel toward you is more than friendly."

Eric pulled her tight to him, needing time to gather his skyrocketing emotions. "Me, too. But I still don't need to know."

She wrapped her arms as tightly around him. "What if I need to tell you before we can go on. So you know the whole me?"

"Then I need to know." Her hair tickled his nose, and he buried his face in its softness. He thought he already had a good idea of the whole Amanda. And he liked what he knew.

She pulled away just enough to look up at him. "I loved him. My college instructor."

"I would expect that. Or you wouldn't have

accepted his proposal," Eric said to cover the discomfort her saying loved had caused him. The only alternative was to kiss her senseless, so she'd forget the past and think only of him. He might be clumsy understanding women and feelings, but even he knew that wasn't the right action, as compelling as it was.

"I loved him until I popped into his office and saw him holding his wife, his pregnant wife, in his arms. His betrayal, the reality of his other life devastated me." She cleared her throat. "I'd never felt so much for a man before, and I haven't since. But I'm beginning to feel that way about you."

Eric lost all ability to breathe. "I …" He struggled to finally drag air into his lungs. "I have a confession, too. I don't know if I've ever truly loved a woman or had one truly love me, plain old Eric Slade, not Eric Slade star, or for what I could do for, give to, them."

Amanda's lips parted as if to speak.

He placed his finger on them, giving himself a nanosecond to feel their softness. "Let me finish. My first wife, Chris's mother, I thought I loved her and her me. But when everything fell apart, I wondered if it might have simply been teenage hormones between us. After that, all my romantic relationships were more of a game, where we both knew the rules." He rested his forehead against hers. There. That didn't paint him in a good light. But it was the truth, and Amanda needed to know it.

"And what are we?" Her voice was a whisper on the ocean breeze.

"Not a game," he said truthfully. "But if we were a game, I'd be losing."

THEIR CONFESSIONS MADE, they walked a couple more steps. "Good to the 'not a game'," Amanda said. "Because I won't be a game, unless I know I am, so I can put my defenses up and play the game."

"No need. I can think of better things for you to use your energy for."

He pressed his lips to her forehead, filling her mind with some of those better things.

She cleared and lifted her head. "I need to ask two things of you."

The expression that flickered across Eric's face verged on terror. She pressed her lips together not to smile. "No subterfuge in our relationship, and what we're doing for each other for the pretend-relationship agreement stays out of the real one. To be blunt, don't try to buy my affections."

Seriousness replaced the terror on his face. "I'll do my best."

"That's all a woman can expect."

He tipped her chin back with his finger. "Shall we seal that with a kiss."

"I thought you'd never ask."

As he dipped closer, the brilliant oranges and reds of the sun setting on the ocean silhouetted Eric's features. Then his lips touched hers and she closed her eyes and let her emotions and his obvious skill take over.

Finally, the squawk of a seagull brought her back to the beach.

He lifted his head and blinked. Several times. "I don't know about you," he said in a gravelly tone. "But that rocked."

She shot him a smug look. "Thank you." She stepped back beside him and slipped her hand in his.

He tilted his head. "That's it. Nothing for me?"

"Nope." Even though she would have sunk into the sand if he hadn't had his strong arms tightly around her. "Your ego is big enough as it is."

"Okay, I'll take that as it rocked you, too."

She laughed. "Exactly what I mean. Now, we'd better get back to work."

"Work?"

"Yes, the important work of making sure the Indigo Bay holiday decorations are up to snuff."

"What do we do if we find an undecorated cottage or house? Hand out a citation?"

"Of course not. I just like to see all the houses and business bright and sparkly. Look." She pointed down the beach at a row of decorated cottages. "Dallas has all his cottages decorated, even the unrented ones."

Eric looked at her, rather than where she was pointing. "Dallas? The guy at Caroline's."

"Yeah, Caroline's son."

"You weren't, uh …"

She smiled at him. "Involved?" The womanly power that sluiced through her beat what she'd felt when she'd been declared the winner in the mayoral election. "I do declare. You aren't going all jealous on me, are you?"

"Me. Eric Slade?" He met her tease. "Never."

She squeezed his hand. She had no doubt the *actor* didn't feel that emotion, unless required to in his role. The man, on the other hand, she was learning that he was a whole other story.

They walked the beach listening to the sounds of the night. Eric dropped her hand and scooped up a soccer ball that blew across their path. The cottage they were in front of had a kid's bike and other toys on the deck.

He tossed the ball back and forth between his hands. "Shall we do your mayoral duty and return this property to the owner?" Eric grabbed her hand and tugged her toward the cottage, which didn't have any decorations or outside lights on.

"Okay. We can put it up by the stairs. I don't want to disturb them."

When they reached the steps, an attractive woman around her age stepped out. Amanda didn't know her. She had to be new to town or a holiday vacationer.

"Can I help you?" she asked.

Before Amanda could introduce herself, a boy who looked to be about ten darted around the woman and onto the deck.

"Mom! Do you know who that guy is? It's Eric Slade. Remember the sign? It said he was here."

"I'm sure it's … The woman turned on the flood light. "Eric Slade," she said almost reverently.

"In the flesh," he said.

"I've seen all your movies," she gushed.

Amanda clenched her teeth. If the woman had, she was picturing the same shirtless Eric in-the-flesh picture she was.

"We found this soccer ball on the beach," Eric said. "Yours?"

The boy glanced around the deck. "Yeah. If I go get a magic marker, will you sign it?"

"Sure."

"I'm sorry, I didn't introduce myself," Amanda said into the lull in conversation the boy's departure left. "Amanda Strickland, Indigo Bay's mayor."

"Kassie Martin," she said more to Eric than to Amanda. "Eric Slade. I still can't believe it."

"Yeah. Amanda and I were checking out the holiday decorations."

While she appreciated him bringing her into the conversation, this would have been a perfect time for him to put his arm around her. Foster the appearance that they were a couple.

Kassie pushed her long flowing blond hair back from her face. "We just moved in. I'll be teaching at the high school after the holiday break. And haven't had a chance to put up the decorations, Dallas, the landlord gave us." She looked up at the roof peek, similar to Amanda's cottage. "I'm not sure if Jaden and I could handle it by ourselves."

Amanda prided herself on not snorting. She'd decorated her cottage by herself several Christmas seasons.

"I could come over one morning and help," Eric said. "Amanda and I did her cottage in an afternoon."

"Would you, really? I didn't know who to ask."

"You could have asked Dallas. He's single and free," Amanda mumbled under her breath, glad that Jaden's tromping down the stair negated any chance of Eric hearing her.

Jaden handed the marker to Eric, who signed the ball with a flourish. "There you go."

"Thanks." Jaden took the ball and raced up the stairs past his mother with an "I'm going to text the guys."

"His friends at his old school," Kassie said. "How does tomorrow morning sound for the decorations?"

"Should be fine. About 10:00?" Eric called up to her.

Amanda rubbed the toe of her mother's tennis shoe in the sand. *Ah.* So she wasn't invited. He knew she'd be working then. She had mayoral office hours and her other work. Not that Kassie had asked for her help.

"Mom, I forgot the password to your phone," Jaden shouted from inside.

"I've got to go. See you tomorrow, Eric. Nice to meet you, Amy." Kassie waved to them.

Eric slipping his arm around her waist as they walked back toward the shoreline took the sting out of Kassie not remembering her name.

"Is it always like that when people recognize you?"

He raised his gaze to the sea. "Too often."

"How do you take it."

"I have a role I assume for that. And one for interviews. And one for the women who I want to discourage from falling all over me."

Amanda playfully slugged his shoulder, then rubbed her knuckles, surprised at the jolt.

"Ouch! What was that for?"

"Should I be worried?" she asked rather than answering.

"About all the women?" He tried to tickle her side.

"Ha! I'm not ticklish. "No, should I be worried about you and whether you suffer from a multi-personality disorder?"

"Not at all. I'm always Eric, and for you I'm always trying to be my real self."

Despite his light tone, his words knocked her more off balance than her fist bouncing off his rock-solid shoulder.

To cover her skittering control over her emotions, she slid her arm around his waist, too. And pinched his side with her forefinger and thumb. Eric bent over and lurched away.

"I might not be ticklish, but I know someone who is," she chimed, wiggling her fingers.

"Oh, no you don't." He took off at a jog.

She raced after him. He stopped at the last cottage, just short of the Mansion B&B beach, and caught her in his arms.

Amanda bent over, laughing until she felt Eric's stillness. He turned her around in his arms and stared.

"What are you doing?"

"Admiring you. The way the moonlight plays on your hair. Your skin that looks so soft I have to touch it." He ran his finger over her cheek and down her jaw line.

She didn't even try to hide her shudder.

"Yes," he said, crushing her to him before he lowered his lips to hers. Teasing, tasting first, nearly driving her crazy before giving her what she silently cried for, a deep, probing possessive kiss that made the roaring in her ears louder than the waves crashing behind her.

She didn't know how long they stood intwined before he gradually broke the kiss, only that it wasn't long enough.

"I, hem, we'd better get on with our Seaside Boulevard tour, Mayor Strickland."

"Yes, we should, Mr. Slade." She brushed the front of his t-shirt she'd had clenched in her hands. "So that's the real you, not some replay of a movie scene."

"Yes, ma'am. More real than even I knew."

If that was the case, she didn't care how many women threw themselves at him, as long as he kept the real Eric for her.

# CHAPTER 9

Eric stood on the ladder he'd had to borrow from Jeff and plugged in the last string of lights on Kassie's rented cottage and glanced at her sitting below him. Unlike, Amanda, Kassie's participation in the decorating had been limited to pointing at the box of lights Dallas had left in a closet. So it had taken him twice as long, which may have been the idea. He frowned at Kassie, sitting in the sun sipping a drink while her son tried to help between asking 100 questions.

As he started down the ladder, he caught a flash of someone jogging up the beach. *Jeff.* Eric speeded up his descent. "Hey," he called and waved, startling Kassie. He met Jeff on the beach in front of the cottage.

"Hey," Jeff said. "I'm on lunch break from the shop, and Sonja sent me to invite you to join us."

"You're a savior."

"Tough work?"

"I've got a ten-year-old firing nonstop questions and a strange woman watching my every move. I don't mind women admiring me in my movies. It's creepy in person."

Jeff snorted. "Since when?"

"Since …" He stopped himself from finishing *Amanda*. "I don't remember Chris doing the 100 questions." He deflected Jeff's question, he hoped.

"I remember Jesse. Irritated the heck out of me when I was trying to get work done. Then, I missed it when he hit his silent teens."

A pang gutted Eric. He knew his friend hadn't done it purposely, but Jeff had reminded Eric of how little time he'd spent with Chris when he was growing up. "Help me grab your ladder and my tools."

The men climbed the steps to the deck.

"Kassie, this is Jeff Brewster."

"Ah, the childhood friend who brings you to Indigo Bay."

"That and other things."

"Your B&B looks beautiful from outside."

"It's my wife's actually, and she's made it just as beautiful inside. The Barks and Bows Gala a week from Saturday is being held there."

"I've seen the signs."

"Have you bought a ticket?" Jeff asked. "It would

be a great way for you to meet people and see the mansion."

Kassie's gaze moved from Jeff to him and back. "I haven't. I have Jaden. No one to watch him. We're planning on coming to the tree lighting, though."

"Well if you want to go to the gala, too, I'll give you my daughter-in-law's card. She has the law office on Seaside Boulevard." Jeff reached in his back pocket and produced one. "She's got someone lined up to watch my granddaughter. What's one more?"

Kassie fingered the card. "Thanks, I'll think about it. And Eric, the lights look great."

He hadn't noticed that she'd plugged them in when he was talking to Jeff on the beach. "No problem. Glad to be of help."

The guys collected the ladder and tools and headed toward the B&B with Eric uncomfortably feeling Kassie's gaze drilling into his back. "Nice selling job on the gala."

Jeff made an exaggerated bow. "You could have clenched it with an invitation."

"Don't I know. Fortunately, I already have a date."

"Let me guess. Our good mayor."

"Bullseye."

"Just remember, Amanda is Sonja's friend. My friend."

"Heh, what do you expect me to do to her?"

Jeff raised an eyebrow. "The usual?"

"Seriously? Not a chance. We're friends, too. I like her and she likes me."

"Which you?"

"The one you and Sonja invite to visit. Amanda and I are going to see where things go."

"Then, you my friend," Jeff said with a broad grin, "are in big trouble."

Eric mentally made the gesture he might have been scripted to make in one of his movies.

"Amanda. What a surprise," her mother said as Amanda knocked on the screen door and walked into the kitchen. "Just in time for lunch."

"That was the plan. It's such a warm, sunny day again for December, I decided to play hooky from work and come over when I finished at city hall to help you get your outside decorations up." Amanda glanced outside, trying not to be too obvious about checking for Eric's bike, which was parked by the garage. Maybe he was upstairs washing for lunch. Or maybe she should just turn off the where-is-Eric Geiger counter.

Her mother busied herself placing sandwiches and potato salad on the table. "I'll make more for Eric when he gets back."

"He's still helping that woman with her decorations?" *It shouldn't have taken them all morning.*

"He is as far as I know." Her mother pulled out a chair to join her, then turned away to the counter when her cell phone rang. "Eric," she said as she picked up the phone.

Her mother quickly ended the call, and Amanda tapped her foot on the floor while she waited for her to sit and say something.

"Eric's having lunch with Sonja and Jeff, so I'm doubly glad you popped in. To eat the extra sandwiches."

Amanda finished the bite of sandwich she'd taken. "Always glad to help, speaking of which, I won't take no for an answer about putting up your Christmas decorations."

For as long as she could remember, her mother always had everything inside and out decorated the first week of December. But her mother had kept putting it off this year whenever Amanda offered to help her.

"You must be a mind reader. That's what Eric and I have planned for this afternoon."

Amanda took another bite of sandwich to hide her smile at spending the afternoon with Eric, too. *Mom could be a little too intuitive sometimes.*

They were finishing the dishes when Amanda heard a motorcycle drive up the street and turn into the drive. Moments later, Eric walked in.

"Jeff dropped me off," he said.

Amanda placed the two plates she'd dried in the cupboard. He was dressed as he'd dressed to help her decorate, as she'd thought he dressed for her. A muscle shirt and those well-worn jeans that fit him just right. "Dallas must have left a lot of decorations." Her attempt to make her comment sound off-hand sounded exactly like what it was—petty fishing for why he'd been at Kassie's all morning.

"Not really. But she didn't help. Just watched me. The whole time. Jeff saved me with Sonja's lunch invitation. I think Kassie was about to offer me lunch."

His complaining voice boosted Amanda's spirits. "Poor boy. Are you too worn out to help Mom and me with her decorations?"

"I'm never too tired for you two ladies. But first let me tell you about the sales job for the gala that Jeff did on Kassie."

"Good for him," Amanda said when Eric finished. "Sometimes I think the transplants to Indigo Bay are more gung-ho on our town than the long-time natives are."

"I heard that," her mother said, clarifying for Eric, "I'm Indigo Bay born and bred. I'm just a little behind on some holiday stuff this year. Although, I do have a gala ticket. And why are we just standing here talking?" She clapped her hands. "Let's get with it. Amanda, you and Eric get the outside decorations from the garage, and I'll get the inside ones from the attic."

Amanda walked Eric the short distance to far door of the two-car garage.

"I'd about given up on getting her into the holiday spirit," she said as he opened the door. "Mom's always loved Christmas but didn't seem to care this year. Your being here has been good for her."

Eric turned, grabbed her hand, and pulled her around the wall between the doors and into his arms. "How about you? Am I good for you, too?"

"The jury's still out on that one." Despite her words, she made no effort to move out of his arms.

"How's a guy to behave when you're around and not lending any help?"

Amanda swallowed hard when she realized he'd loosened his embrace, but she was still standing just as close.

"I've been a regular Santa's elf," he continued, "helping all the single ladies of Indigo Bay get their decorations up."

No way could she picture Eric as an elf, aside from the twinkle he had in his eye. Even that reminded her more of a little devil than an elf. She lifted her head to him, and he leaned toward her. Her heart started pounding. She lowered her eyelids. And Eric gave her a peck on the tip of her nose.

"So, where are these decorations?" he asked starting across the mostly empty garage.

Her eyes opened and she summoned her voice from the center of her chest where it was caught. "Better watch it. You sounded like you had such fun this morning, that I might just recommend your decorating skills to the fundraising committee. It could be a last-minute money raising appeal to the single women of Indigo Bay."

Eric choked.

She rushed over and patted him on the back. "It could be combined with the donation couch-surfing idea I had."

He bent over in laughter. "I'm going to get you for that."

She grinned. "I can't wait. As for the decorations, they're in the boxes along the far wall."

Eric straightened and faced the wall. "All…" He stopped. "Ten of them?"

"Yep. We have lights for the house and the front yard trees. Lit reindeer and angels. And don't forget the blow-up Santa and Mrs. Claus, Frosty, and the Grinch. Mom has had some of them for a long time."

"Dare I ask what's in the box marked fragile?"

"The most important decoration of all. The manger and ceramic figures for the porch. I'll take care of that."

"You guys have everything covered. I probably

shouldn't tell you that I've gone some years without even a tree."

"Nope, and don't tell me that when you've entertained over the holidays, you've paid an interior designer to decorate."

Eric stacked three boxes and picked them up, peering around the side. "I supposed I shouldn't tell you that I've gotten a couple of those professional house decorations for free."

"Not if you want to score any points with me."

"Score. Hmm."

Heat rushed through her. Her own fault. She was the one who'd said score.

"Not even if I said free for the publicity of having done my house."

She picked up the box with the creche. "Button it and follow me." It made a big difference, but she wasn't going to say that. He had enough of an upper hand with her emotions already.

ERIC STOOD on the front porch, arm draped casually over Amanda's shoulder, surveying the reindeer dancing among the decorated trees, a solemn line of angels, and swaying blow-up characters. "Nice."

Amanda leaned her head on his shoulder. "It'll be spectacular when it's lit up in the dark."

"Nice view here, too."

Amanda stirred, but didn't lift her head. "Yes, the manger is really something. An antique, probably. It belonged to my grandparents."

"That, too," Eric said against her hair. "But it isn't really the something I was looking at."

She snuggled against him, and he tightened his arm around her. Then, the screen door creaked, and Amanda jumped away.

"Everything looks wonderful," Lisa said. "Come on in and have a cool drink."

He shook his arm. *Something to cool him down. Good idea.*

"Oh, Mom," Amanda said when she stepped into the living room. "You've outdone yourself."

"I've seen professional jobs that weren't nearly as nice," Eric said.

Beside him, Amanda made a choking, coughing sound. "Excuse me. Dry throat."

"Let's get those drinks. And thanks. I had a good time decorating." Lisa led them to the kitchen. "Sweet tea, or Eric has some beer in the refrigerator."

"Ale," he specified for Amanda. "And I'll take one."

"Me, too," Amanda said.

Lisa started toward the refrigerator.

Eric beat her to it. "Tea for you. Lisa?"

"Yes, please." She took three glasses from the cupboard while he grabbed two bottles of ale with one hand and the pitcher of tea with the other, closing the refrigerator with his elbow.

He placed the tea on the table and opened an ale for Amanda.

She took the bottle and looked at the label. "The good stuff." She picked up her glass and filled it.

He sat and did the same, raising his glass. "Something we have in common."

She smiled over the neck of the bottle.

The brand was a niche one, not a commercially popular one. Even so, the discovery of their mutual like shouldn't warm him as much as it did. Or was the warmth from her smile? He took a long draw of his ale.

"Everything is done, except for the Christmas tree," Lisa announced.

Eric stifled a groan. He hated to admit it, but he was kind of beat and would rather relax—preferably, alone with Amanda—for the evening than decorate a tree.

"Would you two want to run down to one of the corner lots with me to get one?"

Lisa didn't even have the tree yet? He'd figured it was out behind the garage or somewhere else he hadn't seen. He didn't track her comings and goings.

"I'll order pizza," Lisa cajoled.

"It's a tradition. When I was a kid, Mom and I always got pizza when we put up the Christmas tree."

He and his son didn't have many traditions, except one. "The pizza sounds great, so no one has to cook supper. But I have a better idea about the tree."

"Not artificial," Amanda said. "We never do artificial."

"I wouldn't think of it. Have you ever cut your own tree? Chris and I used to. We'd drive out of the city into the mountains, make a day of it." He stopped. "Assuming there's a Christmas tree farm within driving distance."

"There is," Lisa said. "In north Charleston. I got a flyer about it in the mail."

"Perfect. Eric and I have an interview at the Charleston newspaper Thursday morning. We can drive up to the farm afterwards and get both our trees. I've never cut my own before."

"Great. You don't mind not coming, Lisa."

She waved him off. "Not at all."

Eric's phone rang a familiar ring tone. He pushed away from the table. "I should take this. It's Chris."

"Hey, Chris," he said as he stepped into the living room.

"Dad. I'm heading to Jackson Hole. You sure you don't want to join me?"

Eric's stomach knotted. Skiing at Christmastime was their other tradition. And they were going for New Year's. "Sorry, I've made commitments to the folks here … the mayor."

"Amanda Strickland. I've seen the publicity."

He didn't detect any bitterness in his son's voice but blurted out anyway. "I'm not ditching our time together for a woman. I know I've done that too many times before."

"Dad, it's okay."

Eric's heart swelled. Chris did sound okay.

"I'm still coming to Indigo Bay for Christmas, and we have the condo for the week after. And if your 'thing' with the mayor is to discourage Maya, you can call it off. I've taken care of her."

"How?"

"It doesn't matter. Let's just say I had to alleviate my guilt for letting her through the house gates a couple times. Juvenile. I know."

"Thanks for fessing up. I suspected you had. You're sure about Maya being taken care of?"

"Positive."

"Thanks triple for that." Eric rubbed the back of his neck. "About Amanda. You were dead on about us staging a fake holiday romance to ward off Maya's stalking. But it's more than that now."

"Serious, huh?"

"I'd like it to be if I can manage not to mess it up. I have Jeff coaching me."

"Not a bad idea." Chris laughed.

"I can't wait for you to get to know her."

"Looking forward to meeting a woman who has you as uncertain of your prowess as us mortal men."

Chris cleared his throat. "If I wouldn't be imposing, is it okay if I bring someone, uh, special with me?"

"Ha! Cupid got you, too. Those little arrows sting, don't they? No problem. Bring your lady."

"Thanks, Dad. We'll see you Christmas Eve."

"Bye, son."

Eric stared at his phone screen. *It was so simple. How to get on with his son.* Treat Chris like the man he was and not be so fixed on making up for what they missed when he was a kid.

He wasn't sure how, but he was sure knowing Amanda was behind his epiphany. Unlike any other women he'd known, she made him a better man.

# CHAPTER 10

**D**one. Amanda stepped back from her kitchen table and admired her work. All her holiday shopping was done, and gifts wrapped. She frowned. Except Eric's. Sonja and Lauren had kidnapped her from her office for an afternoon of shopping. They'd hit every store in Indigo Bay, and Amanda hadn't found the perfect gift she wanted to give Eric. The problem was that she didn't know what that gift was. She'd been certain it would hit her on their shopping spree. But it hadn't.

Her phone rang, flashing Eric on the screen. "Hi." She hadn't talked to him all day.

"Hi, missed you today."

"Me, too. Mom kept you busy on the house all day?"

"I kept me busy. There's a lot I'd like to get done, but it's hard to juggle the work with all the holiday appearances I'm getting pulled into. I'm supposed to be vacationing."

Guilt erupted inside her. She, Mom, and others *were* asking a lot of him. Especially her since he'd mentioned his conversation with Chris and that the need for a publicized fake holiday was gone. "I can ask mom to lighten up on the house repairs."

"I don't mind the house stuff. I find working with my hands more relaxing than being Eric Slade on stage for the citizens of Indigo Bay."

That was her. "I'm sorry."

"No, I'm being grumpy. It's all for good causes, Christmas and the animal shelter, and usually, like tomorrow, I get to spend time with you."

Amanda went all squishy inside.

"Now, don't tell anyone, but I'm so beat I'm going to go sack out, even though it's only 9:45."

"Our secret. Sweet dreams."

"Only the sweetest with your voice as the last thing I hear before I sleep."

As corny as they sounded, Amanda didn't doubt the sincerity in his words and held that in her heart. "Goodnight."

"'Night, love." Eric clicked off, adding one more thing—was he saying he loved her?—to the stack of things piled up against her having sweet dreams.

She was nervous about the interview tomorrow on top of her general anxiousness to make this the best Indigo Bay Christmas yet. Spending time with

Eric had cut into her mayoral and work duties. To add to her angst, after Public Works and Highway had finally worked out their money sharing, Public Works ran into some problems. The sewage line wasn't completely replaced yet.

Amanda cleaned up her wrapping scraps and went to bed with "`night, love" humming in her head and heart. While that didn't give her sweet dreams, it did stop her from tossing and turning, so she woke up rested and ready to go.

She'd picked out a turquoise sleeveless sheath with enough of a blue to its color to bring out the blue in her eyes and woven straw wedge heels with a faux turquoise stone on the arch band—which reminded her of Lucille. The dress had a matching long-sleeved bolero jacket. Amanda had also tucked leggings, tennis shoes, and her favorite Christmas sweater in a canvas bag for their Christmas tree adventure.

Just as she finished her makeup with a dab of fragrance behind each ear, her phone pinged an email. From the head of Public Works. She hadn't planned on checking email this morning. Her finger waivered over the phone before she opened it. The subject line said, "Good News." She perched on the edge of the bed and smiled as she read. The crew had stayed late yesterday and finished the sewer line replacement. They were opening it to the Mansion

B&B, Public Beach, and the unoccupied cottages this morning.

With a bounce in her step, she went out to her SUV and realized she had no idea if two trees would fit in it. *Two steps forward; one step back.* Maybe Mom's bike rack would fit the vehicle, and they could carry one tree on the roof. She tossed her canvas bag on the back floor and her purse on the front seat console and headed to her mother's.

Eric met her as she got out of her vehicle at her mother's. Was he as anxious to get going and get this over with as she was?

"Hi, right on time."

She gave him a quick once over. Sports jacket, t-shirt, jeans—not the well-worn ones she liked so much, but not new, either—and his black motorcycle boots. Amanda felt over dressed and, all the more uncomfortable. "Hi. I'm not sure two trees will fit in my car, so I want to grab the bicycle roof carrier from the garage just in case."

He nodded. "You look nice."

"Too much?"

"For tree cutting yes. . ."

"I have other clothes in the car," she cut in.

"For the interview, perfect. Professional but feminine, and a little sexy."

Amanda's face heated. "Thank you. That wasn't *exactly* what I was looking for."

"Works for me." He grinned and she wanted to fan herself. "Where's the bike carrier? I'll get it."

"It should be along the back wall." Amanda took the time he was gone to do some deep breathing, take advantage of the slight cool breeze, and listen to the birds singing. She was ready when Eric returned.

"Should I put it on now?" he asked, taking off his jacket and slinging it over his shoulder.

"Let's wait and see if we need it." *Since what I don't need is to watch you and your muscles at work putting it on the car.*

"Okay. You driving?"

"I thought I would."

He hopped in the passenger side. "I knew you would."

She got in her side and stuck out her tongue. "Smarty. I like things under control. But I don't have to control everything."

"True." He drew the word out in his deepest voice.

She shivered at what she couldn't control.

The drive was uneventful, and the feature writer met them in the newspaper lobby as soon as they checked in. After introductions, she took them to a conference room.

"Thank you for coming here," she started. "Indigo Bay would have been better. I'd have had an opportunity for pictures. But we feature writers are all on tight schedules. The drive, you know."

"No problem," Amanda said. "City hall can provide you with pictures of the festivities underway already, leading up to Christmas."

"Fine. We need them no later than Saturday morning." The writer turned to Eric. "So what brings you to our part of the country? Scouting for a new movie?"

Amanda folded her hands on the table. She'd thought Eric told his PR people to stress to the paper Eric's Indigo Bay holiday connection.

Eric's lips thinned before they spread into a wide smile and Amanda witnessed him transforming from Eric the friend to Eric the star. "Friends," he answered, talking about his and Jeff's lifelong friendship, the Mansion B&B, his pitching in to help residents put up their decorations, the animal shelter fundraising.

Amanda sat, feeling more and more like the arm ornament she'd teased him about being the evening they'd gone to the Sweet Caroline's Café. She did appreciate Eric's efforts to direct the writer to her for answers, even though the writer turned them right back to him.

"Will those attending the gala get to see Maya London, too?"

Amanda's stomach sank, and anger flashed on Eric face long enough for her to see it, even if the writer hadn't.

"No, why would they?" he asked pleasantly. "I'll be escorting my good friend, Amanda."

The way he'd said, "good friend Amanda," almost as a caress had her heart pounding and her stomach churning.

She was in trouble. She couldn't tell if he was being her Eric or star Eric.

THE WRITER WAS STOMPING on his last nerve. Granted, she was writing a feature, not hard news. But this was a respected news outlet not Twitter or some tabloid rag. His PR person was going to get an earful when he and Amanda were done here.

"And if people need a further enticement to scoop up tickets to the Barks and Bows Gala … " He looked at Amanda. "I'm donating a day for two on the North Carolina set of my next movie with paid accommodations the nights before and after to the gala's silent auction." He crossed his arms, leaned back in his seat, and gave the info on getting tickets.

"That should wrap things up," the writer said.

Amanda touched his arm, and he could barely cover the jolt it caused. He was tenser than he'd thought.

"There's also the Indigo Animal Shelter preadoption clinic and shelter tours," she said. "People can adopt pets to bring into their homes after the holidays. Eric will be there all Tuesday afternoon."

"With the mayor," he added.

"I'm good." The feature writer powered off her tablet. "The story will be in the paper Wednesday in our special holiday-doings regional section."

Eric and Amanda thanked her and said goodbye.

"Let's blow this place," he said as they walked down the hall to the lobby.

Amanda slowed at the Ladies Room and lifted her canvas bag. "I want to change for the tree cutting."

"We can stop someplace on the way for you. I don't like interviews anyway, and that writer got on my nerves. We were there to talk about an Indigo Bay Christmas."

Amanda unlocked the SUV and they got in. "Is that why you got so public about us? Because you were angry at the writer?"

His chest tightened. "That's what you thought? No, I want everyone to know."

Her hand faltered as she pressed the ignition.

"You know when I talked with Chris at your mom's?"

"Yeah." She pulled onto the street and headed north.

"I was waiting until today when we were alone to tell you. He said Maya is all taken care of. She's moved on. We don't have to pretend anymore. Don't have to make up some amicable breakup after the holidays."

Amanda chewed her bottom lip.

*Not a good sign.* "What did I do?"

She sighed. "It … we're still so new. I thought we could let ourselves get used to it. Give ourselves a little time for our relationship just to be ours. Time to break it to Mom. I don't know. Talk with Sonja."

He put his hand on her thigh, and she didn't push him away. I think your mother already has a pretty good idea, and I talked with Jeff. Sonja probably does, too. Is that so bad?"

"No." She shook her head.

He released a pent-up breath. Jeff had warned him about messing things up.

"It's just that you rushed ahead and announced it to the feature writer. Put us out there, bigger than life."

"Aw, come on." He squeezed her leg, gaining a hint of a smile. "Admit it, bigger than life is what you like about me."

Amanda sobered and pulled into a fast food restaurant. "No, I don't need bigger than life from you. I just need plain old *you*." She shut down the engine and squeezed his hand.

Now, if that didn't just make him want to shout from the rooftops in elation and bury his head in the sand at the same time.

She opened her door. "Would you order me an Italian half-sub and tea while I change?"

"Sure." They entered the restaurant. She went toward the Ladies Room and he to the counter.

A few minutes later, he watched her walk to the table where he sat with their order. She was wearing what could be described only as an award-winning ugly Christmas sweater. His mouth went dry. And black form-fitting leggings tucked into black leather boots. The back of his neck prickled, and he glanced around the place. To him, every male from teens on up appeared focused on Amanda. He gritted his teeth until she sat across from him, those legs safely hidden under the table.

"That's some sweater," he said shading his eyes as if the sparkles and spangles were blinding him.

She smiled. "I thought you'd like it."

*Not nearly as much as the leggings and boots.*

Before he could say anything, a teen boy interrupted, "You *are* Eric Slade."

It was on the tip of his tongue to deny the boy, when Amanda said, "Yes, he is."

He shot her *I'll-get-you-for-this daggers.*

She laughed. "Now we're even. You outed us, and I outed you." She bit into her sub.

The teen looked bewildered. "Could I, uh, have your autograph?" He shoved a piece of paper and a pen at him.

"Certainly." Eric took the pen. "Your name."

"Aidan."

He scrawled a message and his signature across the paper. "Do you have a phone? How about a picture of us?"

"Yes." Aidan fumbled to pull his phone out of his back pocket.

Eric stood and nodded at Amanda. "Would you?"

She took the phone from the teen and Eric offered Aiden his signature fist bump.

"Got it," she said returning the phone.

Aiden looked at it. "Cool." He scooped up the autograph. "Thanks."

Eric and Amanda sat. "You know, it used to be the young ladies that flocked to me for autographs. Now it's teen boys."

"Poor baby." She patted his hand.

"I don't mind. Not now that I've got you."

"Think you've got me, do you?"

Why had he said that out loud?

"You do."

Even he had enough finesse to know he shouldn't go with his first instinct to pull her from her chair and kiss her senseless. Instead, he lifted her hand, turned it over, and kissed her palm.

The satisfaction he got from her misty eyes and dewy expression was almost as good as kissing her senseless.

# CHAPTER 11

"We'd better get this show on the road. We have two perfect Christmas trees to find and cut," Amanda said, as soon as she could find her voice. A voice she couldn't keep the shake out of.

"Yes, we do." Eric cleared their table and returned to offer his arm.

Amanda hesitated, not sure she could take the unsettling consequences of touching him. She mustered her strength and slipped her arm through his.

Settled in the car, she said, "I'm glad we don't have to keep up the fake romance pretense anymore, but you have to promise me one thing."

"Your wish is my command."

She punched the ignition. "I'm serious. Promise me you won't drop any publicity bombs I don't know about ahead of time."

"You have my word. I'm sorry my execution of my earlier promise was a little sloppy. I got carried away by my feelings. Can I have a retake?"

Her determination to have her say softened, but only slightly. "I have to be able to trust you if we're going to be anything more than a holiday romance."

His gaze held hers with what looked like panic in his eyes. "I'll do my best."

She broke eye contact and put the vehicle in reverse to pull out of the parking spot. Normally, she would have said that was all she could ask. But the tremor in his voice. It had to be acting. No way she could have affected him that much. Amanda shoved the gearshift into drive and accelerated more than she'd meant to.

Eric sat silent beside her until they were on the highway, and then all he said was, "My phone directions say the tree farm turnoff is eight miles up on the right."

"Thanks." She couldn't think of anything else to say. Maybe the moment would pass.

"There," he pointed ahead seven minutes later.

She knew because she'd involuntarily been timing the silence.

"The sign. Do you see it?" he asked.

That broke the ice wall between them. She laughed. "How could I miss it. It's a 25-foot sign with neon green and red flashing lights shaped like a cookie cutter Christmas tree."

He responded with a lopsided smile that went straight to her heart. "I am trying. To be just plain old Eric Slade. Seriously. But I'm a little rusty."

"You're forgiven." She turned and drove down the sideroad to a parking lot next to a log cabin and rows of fir trees as far as she could see. She took his hand when they met in front of her SUV on the walkway by the cabin. It was a little clammy. Again, she was startled at her effect on him.

"It seems weird to be doing this without snow," he said as entered the cabin.

"Okay surfer guy, you're not going to tell me your Southern California beaches have any more snow than my South Carolina beaches."

"No, I'm not. Chris's maternal grandparents had a cabin in the mountains east of Los Angeles. We got our trees near there. I always tried to choose a day when there was snow. Good times." His expression animated as if he was seeing the mountains, the snow, his son as a child. "They still let me bring Chris after his mother and I split."

"I've never been in the mountains in winter," she said.

"Then we have something to do next Christmas. The property I bought in North Carolina for shooting movies goes up into the mountains, and some of the acreage used to be part of a Christmas tree farm. The remaining trees aren't too tall yet. We can go cut our next year's tree there in the snow."

Amanda was glad they'd reached the check-in counter so she could casually lean on it until her knees turned back into a solid substance. Eric was talking about *them* next year cutting *their* Christmas tree.

Maybe she had been a little quick to jump to conclusions. Maybe Eric *was* trying his best to not fall back on acting and practiced actions when pressed by their relationship.

But, then she was doing her best, too, not to let the protective wall she built around her heart since grad school be insurmountable for either of them.

"HI, FOLKS," an older man greeted them over the counter. "Are you here for a cut tree or to cut a tree?"

Eric tugged the brim of his ball cap he'd put on when he'd gotten out of the car a little lower, glad that he'd stuck it in his back pocket. Maybe if he'd worn it in the restaurant, the kid wouldn't have recognized him. Maybe Amanda wouldn't have brought up his gaffe at the news interview.

"We definitely want to cut one." He turned his face toward her. "Can we get a cut one for your mother?"

"I don't know. Let's see how tired you are after one."

"What do you mean, me tired? This is a joint

effort. Let's see how tired you are." Teasing each other. This was how he felt most comfortable. But they had to be serious sometimes.

"You're a lot older than me," she taunted.

The guy behind the counter interrupted, staring at Eric. "That profile. The voice. You're Eric Slade."

He nodded reluctantly.

The man switched his attention to Amanda, eying her a little too closely for Eric. "Should I recognize you, too?"

"I don't know. I'm the mayor of Indigo Bay," she said completely straight-faced.

The man touched his lip and narrowed his eyes. "Indigo Bay. Is that a new movie?"

"No, we're busting on you." Eric checked the man's name tag. "Larry."

"It's the best beach town on the coast," Amanda said.

"And you're the mayor."

"Yes, Amanda Strickland. And if you have any, I'm looking for blue spruce."

*Way to get down to business, Mayor.*

"I'm sorry. We do have some blue spruce, but none left on the lot to cut."

Eric searched Amanda's face to read her disappointment. What he saw was indecision.

"Mom and I really prefer blue spruce, and there's always next year when we can go tree hunting earlier."

His heart slammed against his chest with far more force than it should have at her off-hand remark about them together next year.

"We'll take already cut ones."

"They're out around the back of the cabin. Pick the ones you want and bring the tag in. The guys outside will wrap them for you." Larry cleared his throat. "When you come back in, could I have a picture with you?"

"Sure. And, if you want, I'll take your card and have my people send you an autographed one."

"Thanks, I'll put it on our wall of famous people who have gotten trees here." Larry pointed to the side wall with a photo of someone dressed in a Santa costume and laughed.

"I'll be in good company," Eric said, taking Amanda's hand. *As I am now.*

Around the back of the cabin, Amanda slowly walked the short line of blue spruce leaned against the log wall, while he enjoyed the view. Of her.

She stood one up beside her. "Too tall." Retraced her steps a couple of trees and selected another. "Too short." She replaced the tree and reached for the one next to it.

"What's the verdict, Goldilocks?" he teased, pulling out his phone and snapping a photo. She looked so cute with her nose wrinkled in indecision.

"Just right."

He stepped to her left. "This one looks about the same height." He held it upright on her other side.

She placed her chosen tree on the ground and eyed the one he held. "I'm not sure it's full enough." Amanda brushed a couple of branches that were caught up on others and brushed his side in the process.

He tightened his grip on the tree to control the rush he'd gotten from her touch.

"Yes, this one is good, too."

Eric and Amanda dragged the trees the short distance to the machine that encased trees in net bags. The machine operator took the tags from the tree and handed them to Eric. He and Amanda went inside, and he handed the tags to Larry, who rang them up. He and Amanda almost simultaneously whipped out their wallets.

"I've got this," Eric said, slapping a credit card on the counter.

"Nope," Amanda stood firm. "Mom insisted on giving me money for hers."

"Okay, you pay for your mother's, and I'll pay for yours. An early Christmas gift."

The firm set of her mouth made him think she was going to insist on paying for both. He inched closer and put his arm around her waist. "Okay?"

"Okay." She put her mother's cash on the counter. "Now, how about that picture?" she asked when Larry was done.

While the man walked around the counter, Eric took off the ballcap and ran his hand through his hair.

"You're beautiful," Amanda said.

Larry handed her his phone, and Eric stepped beside him and flung his arm around Larry's should as if they were old buddies.

"Got it," Amanda said after snapping the camera a couple times. "Now, I want one for me. A keepsake of my first almost cut-your-own Christmas tree."

"Do you want one of you two?" Larry asked when she'd finished?

"Yes."

She changed places with Larry and handed over her phone. Eric handed the man his, too, before he put his arm around her waist and pulled her close. He leaned his head against hers.

"Great pose," Larry said as he snapped away.

But it wasn't a pose to him. It was what felt natural. After their conversation in the car, he hoped Amanda felt the same.

They thanked Larry and went out to find that they could fit both trees in the SUV, even with the bike rack in there, too. A few miles into the drive home, Eric slapped his knee. "We didn't have hot chocolate before we left. That's an integral part of tree-cutting."

"But this was an almost-tree-cutting. I have some

cocoa mix at home. We can have some while we decorate my tree."

"You're going to let me decorate your tree? The man who has other people do his decorating?"

"Why not?"

He studied her placid profile with skepticism. "I figure you have some sort of structured plan I'm doomed to mess up."

Amanda simply snorted.

They dropped off her mother's tree and declined Lisa's invitation to supper. On their way to the cottage, he ordered pizza to be delivered. He carried the tree inside when they got there and eyed the box in her living room labeled Christmas ornaments.

"I'll get the tree up and string the lights while you make the hot chocolate. I did that for my mother once I was big enough. Then she decorated the tree."

"Okay."

The tree went up without a hitch. He smiled when he pulled the lights from the box. Eric had expected all white or blue. There were three strings of flashing multi-colored lights and the gaudiest star he'd ever seen to top the tree. Another side to the mayor that he'd only seen hints of before? He tested the strings and found them all working before he went to work himself. A knock sounded on the door as he went to plug the tree in.

"I'll get it," Amanda said, and came back with the pizza. She placed it on the coffee table, went back to the kitchen, and returned with plates, napkins, and the hot chocolate. "Nice job." She nodded toward the tree. "Why don't you reward yourself with some pizza while I hang the ornaments?"

So she did have a method to her decorating. He scarfed down a slice of pizza and sipped his hot chocolate. But darn if he could figure out what the method was. Amanda's placement of the ornaments seemed as random as his would be. As she passed by the table, she took bites of pizza and sips of hot chocolate, until the two of them had finished the food and she had all the ornaments hung.

"Now comes the fun part." She picked up two boxes of icicles from the side table next to the couch.

"Oh, good. Do I get to string them on one at a time with your approval?"

"Hardly." She opened a box, took a good handful, and proceeded to fling it at the top of the tree.

Eric leaped up and grabbed some of his own. "This I can do. Expertly."

They laughed and tossed—over their shoulders, from under a leg, one-handed, two-handed—until both boxes were emptied. Then they collapsed in laughter on the couch.

She caught her breath. "Christmas was one of the times I'd wished I'd had a sibling to share with like this."

Eric's arms trembled as he pulled her to his lap. "The tinsel was fun, but what I feel for you is anything but sibling-like. You know how I said I didn't know if I was capable of loving a woman? I know now. I love you, Amanda. More than anything on earth." Before she could react to his admission, he lowered his head and kissed the only woman he'd ever truly loved

Kissed her until his heart said they were one.

Amanda finished her makeup for work and frowned at her reflection in the mirror. It wasn't that her makeup wasn't applied as skillfully as always or that her hair wasn't just right or that she didn't look as together as she usually did.

The problem was that, despite her cool veneer, her insides were a train wreck. She was doing the acting she'd been so quick to accuse him of after the newspaper interview—which had appeared in yesterday's edition and was all she'd hoped for.

All of this turmoil because of those three little words Eric had said last Thursday. The words that despite the truth that would have been in them, she'd been unable to say back. Instead, she'd burrowed into the warm rightness of being in his arms. And fallen asleep. She'd woken in the early morning hours to find him gone and had headed to the bedroom. But not before she caught the message he'd scrawled on a napkin on the coffee table.

*Sweet Dreams, Love.*

She hadn't slept well in the seven nights since. But she still hadn't brought herself to tell him she loved him, too. Any other time she'd come even close to telling a man she'd loved him, the relationship had headed downhill. She liked what they had and didn't want to endanger it. So she'd managed the situation since then by being busy when he wasn't and not busy when he was, avoiding alone time with him. She placed her elbows on her vanity and cradled her head in her hands.

Eric had taken it all in stride. Amanda lifted her head and smiled in the mirror. He'd acted as if nothing were different, everything was good between them. Maybe he felt the words she believed but couldn't say. Maybe she wouldn't have to risk saying them. She slapped her hands to the arms of her seat and pushed the chair back to leave for work.

*Or*, she grabbed her phone, she should call Eric and tell him. Make both of their days. Before she could decide, the phone rang in her hand. The number of the engineering company she was working with on the 55+ community outside of Myrtle Beach showed on the screen.

"Strickland Architecture. Amanda Strickland speaking."

"Amanda, this is Kelly at Newkirk Engineering."

*The firm's administrative assistant.* "What's up?" Amanda walked downstairs while she talked.

"Dave has had a heart attack."

"Is he all right?" Amanda interrupted.

"He's okay, but we have a new engineer on the project while Dave's recuperating. She's new to the company, so you haven't worked with her before. I know it's short notice, but she wants to meet with all the principals involved in the project here tomorrow morning at nine with a tour of the site progress so far afterwards."

Amanda closed her eyes to visualize her schedule for tomorrow. There was nothing she had to be in the mayor's office for in the morning. "I can clear my schedule for the meeting."

The call paused. "Alicia … Alicia Morales, the engineer would like to meet with you and the developer first this evening over dinner."

"I can do that." Amanda wanted to get any project details that included her to be wrapped up by tomorrow so she could take her planned time off for the holidays.

Kelly gave Amanda a time and a restaurant in Myrtle Beach. "I'll let Alicia know you'll be there."

Amanda hung up, locked the cottage door behind her, and scrapped her plans to walk to city hall today. She needed to get in her full time this morning before she got ready for the three-hour drive to Myrtle Beach.

The dashboard screen lit with a call notification from Eric.

"Hey," she answered. "What's up?"

"If you can spare it, I need your help."

"With what?" she asked tentatively.

"You have to rescue me. Your mother talked me into Christmas ornament painting at Coastal Creations this afternoon. I guess the Tuesday painting maxed out, so they scheduled a second one. And somehow lots of people seemed to know I'll be there."

"That somehow would be Mom. I'm glad to see her getting back to her old self. So what would I be rescuing you from?"

"Embarrassment. The only painting I've ever done is houses and motorcycles."

Amanda laughed and relaxed back in her seat. "And how would I do that?"

"Moral support. You know, hand pats. Good job. That sort of thing."

She laughed harder. "What time?" If it were early afternoon, she could squeeze it in before she had to leave.

"3:00 to 4:00."

She pulled into the city hall parking lot and sat with the car on. Maybe she could see if she could push dinner tonight to 7:00. If she dressed and packed before the painting event, she could leave right after and make dinner.

"Let me see." Amanda stopped. No, she'd be dropping everything and rearranging her work, her life for a guy. She couldn't let herself fall into that pattern again. "I'm sorry. I have an unexpected dinner meeting in Myrtle Beach with the new engineer and the developer of the 55+ project there. Tomorrow morning I'm meeting with the entire project team."

An exaggerated sigh came across her car speakers. "I tried. Think of me struggling to be artistic in a media other than acting while you're having a pleasant drive along the shore."

"You do understand?" She bit her tongue. Her voice sounded so needy.

"Of course. Give me a call from your hotel when you're back from dinner."

"Sure." Amanda stared at the "call ended" message on her dashboard screen. She believed him that he understood.

But why was she so disconcerted by that?

"IF YOU DON'T STOP pacing, you're going to have to replace my living room carpeting along with the other stuff you're finishing here," Lisa said.

Eric checked the clock on the DVR. Nearly 9:00. "She said she'd call after dinner," he mumbled under his breath.

"Sit down." Lisa pointed at the recliner. "If Amanda said she'd call, she'll call. She rarely says something she doesn't mean."

Eric dropped into the chair. Is that why she hadn't returned his I love you? Because she didn't? His phone rang, and he bolted to his feet. "It's Amanda. I'm going to, ah, take it upstairs" He punched the answer button to Lisa's laughter. Why did he feel like he was 15 again with his first real girlfriend?

"Hi," he answered softly. "I was about ready to give up. Ornament painting is exhausting labor. All those ladies crowding around to help the neophyte—me. I could hardly fit them all in in the hour we had to paint."

"Right."

It was so good to hear her voice with her slight southern inflection. Even though they'd talked this morning.

"And how many of those ladies were single and under age 60?"

"So, you're not jealous?"

"How many?"

He could almost hear her tapping her foot. "One. The babe from the cottage I put up the Christmas lights for." No comment from Amanda. He sighed. "And she was there buying jewelry not because I was there. I did have a good talk with Jaden, though. He said my ornament was every bit as good as he could do."

"Poor baby," she soothed.

"How about you. I see it. You stayed late with the handsome engineer who could talk maths with you that I can't even pronounce the name of correctly."

"Yes, we did get into that, but the engineer was much more interested in you."

"You brought me up?" Staking his claim for him? Eric piled the pillows on each other against the bed's headboard and leaned against them, one arm behind his head and the other holding the phone. He crossed his ankles.

"Not exactly. She has 10- and 12-year-old boys and groaned something about having seen all your movies with them. I told her you'd send her boys autographed pictures."

"But how did she know about us if you didn't tell her?"

"Our interview was picked up by one of the wire services from the Charleston paper. She read it in her local paper."

"You're okay with that?"

"It's fine. I have to admit I'm more comfortable with the word getting out to people I don't know than the Indigo Bay grapevine."

"You haven't told anyone yet?"

She scoffed. "Mom said she knew a couple weeks ago. And when Sonja dragged me shopping for a gala gown, and I told her, she said she'd suspected since we continued our friendship beyond last summer."

"So Jeff kept his mouth shut?"

"I'm talking about pouring my heart out to people and that's all you have to say?" she teased.

*I could say you can pour it out to me, too.* But he needed her to say it to him of her own accord, not because he was desperate to hear it.

"Moving on. I missed you. Not only today, but the past week when we've been like ships passing in the night."

"I missed you, too, and I'm all yours now," she said softly.

That was in the direction of what he needed to hear.

"What time do you expect to be home tomorrow?"

"Mid-afternoon, I would hope. I'll text you when I'm leaving with an ETA. Believe me, there's nothing I need more than a relaxing evening at home with you."

She said need, not want. He virtually clasped that to his heart. They chatted a few minutes longer, about what he couldn't say, before she said good night.

"Sweet dreams, love." He couldn't help himself.

But saved from his own lovelorn self again, she'd already ended the call before he'd prompted her declaration.

"I'm going to do it. I'm going to do it tonight," Amanda said aloud to herself in the car for the third or fourth time. She'd stopped on the drive home and picked up a complete cook-at-home gourmet meal for two and an appropriate wine to go with it. Her plan: to clean up and dress in something soft and feminine. Then, as she'd said when she'd texted Eric she was leaving Charleston, she'd let Eric know she was home. Greet him at the door with a glass of wine and a kiss. *Yeah*, that's what she'd do. *Set the mood.*

She passed the Welcome to Indigo Bay sign and turned toward the beach. When she pulled up to her cottage, she blinked and stared. Eric sat on her steps with a bouquet of white camellias she was sure he'd picked himself from her mother's bushes interspersed with red roses. And he didn't think he was artistic?

Eric rose as she stepped out of the car, food and wine in hand, and took in his white dress shirt with the sleeves rolled up on his forearms and black jeans. The shirt fit so perfectly, accentuating his masculine assets, that it had to have been custom tailored.

Heart beating widely, she did her best to glide seductively toward him. She set the bag on the steps beside him and took the flowers. "They're beautiful." She buried her nose in the flowers to smell the roses.

He beamed, and she placed the bouquet next to

the food, reached up, and cupped his face with her hands. She pulled him to her until she could murmur against his lips, "I missed you," before kissing him thoroughly. When she broke away dazed, Eric pulled her tight to him.

"I missed you, too." He returned her kiss just as thoroughly and with more finesse.

"I have food," she said out of nowhere, trying to regain her wits.

"Food is good, but man can't live on bread alone." He shot her a self-satisfied smile.

She didn't care. She felt pretty self-satisfied herself. "Nor can woman."

He picked up the food and bouquet.

She took the flowers. "You're being here when I got home messed up my plan, you know."

They walked up the steps.

"And what plan was that?"

She unlocked the door and they went into the cottage. "I was going to come home and get pretty. Put on a dress I bought when Sonja and I went shopping for our gala gowns…" She pictured the dress—soft cornflower blue fabric with just the right kind of drape to be comfortable and the sexiest thing she owned except her emerald gala gown. "Do my makeup and hair and put our dinner in the oven. Then I was going to let you know I was home."

Eric shrugged. "What can I say? I couldn't wait to see you. You texted me when you left Charleston and

I calculated your travel time. Besides, you don't have to dress up to be pretty. You always are to me."

"Thanks. But I'm going to go ahead with the first part of my plan anyway. Would you put the food in the oven while I change?"

"Sure thing."

"And help yourself to the wine, if you want."

Amanda's hands shook when she put on her earrings and necklace. The final touches to her outfit. She looked good, fantastic even. But she couldn't totally rid her mind of the thought that Eric had his choice of women far more glamorous than her. She steeled her nerves and walked the short hall into the living room. Eric was sitting at the far end of the couch, ankle crossing his knee, arm draped across the couch back sipping wine. Her breath caught. This gorgeous, wonderful man loved *her*.

He glanced at her in the doorway and whistled. "Be still my heart."

She would have laughed except the look in his eyes said he wasn't teasing. Amanda gulped a breath. "You don't clean up badly yourself."

He massaged the back of the couch. "I had a sports jacket on, too, but it was too warm."

Amanda walked to him. "Admit it, you thought the jacket might have detracted from the wow effect of your custom-fitted shirt."

"There is that. Now enough mutual admiration.

Sit with me." He handed her a glass of wine. "Tell me about your trip."

"First and best, everything is fine with the 55+ community project." She sipped her wine. "Sonja reported that the B&B ballroom is decorated beautifully, and the raffle and silent auction items are coming in fast and furious. Everything seems to be falling into place for tomorrow night. Which means I'm officially on vacation from the mayor's office and my firm."

Eric lifted her glass from her hand and placed both glasses on the coffee table. "I'll kiss to that." And he did with a short sweet press of his lips that ricocheted through her almost as strongly as his more passionate kisses.

"Your … your turn," she stuttered. "What were you up to while I was gone?"

"Of course, there was my epic ornament painting. And I squeezed in some time to try to complete the work I'm doing on your mother's house. I just might have to stay through the end of the year if I'm going to finish it all. Join Chris for skiing a week later."

"Don't change your plans for me."

"Even if I want to?"

The heat in his eyes almost melted her into the couch.

"Or you could change your plans…"

She stiffened and caught herself before she thought Eric would notice. They'd have times ahead when they'd need to change plans for each other. It came with the territory of nurturing a relationship. It didn't mean domination.

"And come to Jackson Hole with me for the week between Christmas and New Year's, he finished."

"That's your time with your son. You'll just have to come back as soon as you can to finish Mom's house repairs."

"I'm planning on the coming back—often."

The timer on the stove beeped, breaking the moment.

"Your dinner awaits, my lady." Eric rose and offered his hand and walked her to the kitchen where he'd not only cooked but also set the table. With the candles and candleholders she kept in a kitchen utility drawer for the power outages storms often brought to the coast.

"Lovely," she said.

"Yes, lovely," he repeated as he pulled out a chair and raked his gaze over her as he seated her.

She dug into her meal. "This is delicious. I'm going to have to remember the brand."

His expression was still the same one he'd had when he'd seated her, not the gloat-tinged one she'd expected because he cooked the meal. She took another forkful, chewed, and swallowed. She revised her assessment. It was the company, not the food. Amanda had expected an Eric-the-star reaction and gotten the just-plain-Eric one. Her heart nearly burst from her chest.

They talked over dinner and while they cleared the table, but she'd be hard pressed to say what about.

"What's your favorite chick flick?"

Amanda stared at him. "*Legally Blonde*. Why?"

He slipped her hand in his and walked her to the couch. "I should have known without asking." Eric sat and pulled her down next to him. "I thought we'd watch it. If you don't mind pouring us an after-dinner drink, I'll log into my Prime account and see if it's available there."

"No need. I have the DVD."

"Of course, you do."

While she walked to the DVR and put it on, he poured what was left of the wine they'd had earlier and pulled his cell phone from his pocked and placed it on the table. "More comfortable," he mumbled.

Amanda sat and snuggled close to him. "More comfortable," she repeated. He put his arm around her shoulder and squeezed her closer if that was possible.

About three-quarters through the movie, Eric's phone buzzed, splitting open their cocoon of laughter and love. He glanced at the phone and stiffened before grabbing it and punching end call. He tapped the screen a couple more times.

"Sorry. I have it on do not disturb now." He rolled his shoulders and settled back on the couch.

She nestled close, sensing some tension from the call remaining. Amanda placed her hand on his thigh, and he seemed to relax.

"That was fun," she said, turning the DVR off when the credits started rolling.

"If you think that was fun…" He pulled her onto his lap and his phone rang. "Sorry. That's Chris. I have an exception for his calls. I should take it. A parent, you know, when the kid calls this late."

She didn't know. Not really. Amanda scrambled off his lap with a dread that this was the end of their evening.

What she *did* know was that she still hadn't told Eric she loved him.

"Hey, Chris. What's up?" Eric glanced at her and tightened his fingers around the phone.

Her heart sank. From that and the set of his jaw, now wasn't the time to make any declarations.

# CHAPTER 13

"It's not Chris." Maya's voice came over Eric's phone. "Don't hang up. Chris has been in a skiing accident. I tried to call you earlier. You hung up, and my later calls went to your voicemail. The hospital finally let me have his cell phone to reach you when you didn't respond to their messages."

"How bad is it?"

"Pretty bad, I think. He was unconscious when they took him to the hospital. He's in surgery now. That's all I know. They won't tell me anything. I didn't even know they'd taken him to the hospital until he didn't show up at the condo when he should have."

He swallowed the lump in his throat, but it only went as far as his chest. "And what was he doing skiing this late? It's nearly midnight." Eric needed something to hang his anger at himself on for not taking Maya's call or checking his voicemail. He wasn't even going to think about why Maya had been in the condo.

"The time difference," Maya's voice was subdued.

"You're at the hospital?"

"Of course, I am."

"Let them know I'll call as soon as I have arrangements to be there unless you find out he's out of surgery. Then, I want to talk to the surgeon. Make sure they have this number."

"Okay."

Eric hung up. "Chris was in a skiing accident. He's in surgery. That's all I know." Amanda put her arms around his waist from the back while he fumbled with his phone to call his pilot. He dropped the phone and swore.

"Sit." Amanda pushed him gently toward the couch, picked up the phone, and sat next to him. "What are you trying to do?"

"Call my pilot. But a commercial flight might be faster if Charleston has anything to Jackson Hole early."

He watched Amanda's fingers moving on his phone screen as he hadn't been able to make his move.

"There's one at 6:05 with seats in first class. It arrives in Jackson Hole about 12:30."

He'd recovered enough of his wits to calculate how long it would take his pilot to get from Los

Angeles here and to Jackson Hole. "That's faster than I can do with my plane. Book a seat." He pulled out his wallet and handed her a credit card and his license.

She took them and went to work. "All booked. When do you want to leave? I can swing by Mom's so you can grab some clothes and stuff."

"I'm ready now, but just take me to your mother's. I'll drive my bike. Have Jeff pick it up tomorrow."

"No, I'll take you. I insist. I can book another seat and come with you to Jackson Hole if you need me to."

"Please don't. The bike ride will get my head on straight like a car ride wouldn't. I need to be there for Chris without a woman with me, even the woman I love with all my heart."

"All right," she said after a hesitation that seemed to last for minutes. "But promise me that you'll call or text as soon as you get to the airport and when you get to the hospital."

"I promise, and I love you all the more for understanding about Chris and my breaking our deal and not being here tomorrow..." He glanced at the clock. "Today to escort you to the gala."

"Nonsense about breaking our deal. You've done so much more." Amanda stood, took his hands, and pulled him to his feet to hug him tightly, her head resting on his chest. "So, so much more. I..."

She had to feel, hear his heart pounding against his chest wall as he waited for the words he'd been wanting to hear back from her.

She jumped up from the couch. "I'd better get you over to Mom's." The quiver in her voice and tremble of her lips spoke to him what her words hadn't. They drove to Lisa's in companionable silence.

"Here we are," she said with false cheer when she pulled into her mother's driveway.

He reached for the door handle and stopped. "Aren't you going to walk me to the door?"

She looked at him, and he thought, don't make me say it—say how much I need one more kiss to keep me going tonight.

"Where are my manners. Of course, I'm walking you to the door."

He met her in front of the car. "I can't make it all the way to the door." He pulled Amanda into his arms propelled by the hunger on her face that matched the hunger in him. Their lips met in an equally sparked kiss. When he couldn't get enough of her, he angled his lips for a better taste of her sweetness and lost himself until she squirmed in his arms.

"I don't think we can get any closer," she said.

Her words vibrated on his lips and then through him. He loosened his grip on her, and she looked up, her eyes shining.

"I love you, Eric Slade. So much." She took his

hands and squeezed them. "Safe travel." She squeezed his hands again. "No speeding. Get some sleep in the VIP lounge at the airport. And take my love for you and my prayers for Chris with you."

When she released him, he pressed his hand to his heart unable to do any more than bite his lip and nod to her before he went inside for his things. At the steps, he turned slightly, a request for her to drive him to Charleston on his lips. But she was in the car, no longer watching him. As if she couldn't bear to see him go in as much as he couldn't bear to have her leave.

He lifted his hand in a wave and started up the stairs with the sound of her engine humming behind him. As much as he wanted her with him, he knew she had responsibilities he shouldn't expect her automatically to drop for him. She loved him. That was more than enough. But he still wanted to do something to help make up for him missing the gala.

The bike ride helped to center him, and the plane trip was uneventful. He slept most of the flight, and seven hours later he strode into the St. John's Medical Center well rested, if not any less on edge about Chris. He went directly to information.

"I need information about Chris Slade."

The woman behind the desk stared at him mute.

"I'm his father."

"You're, you're Eric Slade."

"Yes." Hadn't he just said that?

"He's been moved to progressive care." She gave him the room number and directions before picking up a pad and pen. "Could I …"

"Not now. Maybe later." He turned and headed to the elevator, not caring if he'd been rude.

"Dad," Chris said when he pushed open the door to the room.

"Chris." His son didn't look too bad, aside from the full leg cast, IV, and shadows under his eyes. "What happened?"

Chris looked sheepish. "I was flying down the mountain, perfect snow. Then I wasn't. I woke up here. You didn't have to interrupt your plans and come."

"Yes, I did." Eric walked around the end of the bed to the visitor chairs and noticed Maya. He'd been so focused on checking on Chris, he hadn't even noticed her. "What are you doing here?"

"She's with me, Dad. I told you on the phone. I took care of things. Took her off your hands, so to speak."

Eric glanced from his son to Maya. Chris was grinning. Maya looked more like she wished she could fall through the floor.

"I'll let you two talk." Maya rose. "But first. I apologize for stalking you. It was kind of my agent's idea. Keep myself in front of you so you'd think of me for your next movie."

"You need a new agent. Got a pen and paper?"

She produced them from her bag, and Eric wrote something. "My agent. Contact her tomorrow. I'll text her today to expect your call."

"Thank you." She stepped forward with her arms out as if to hug him and stopped.

Eric opened his arms and gave her a fatherly hug. "No more stalking," he admonished.

"No more stalking. Promise. Not that pursuing you was hard. You're pretty hot for an older guy, but I prefer Chris. We have more in common."

Eric willed himself not to laugh. She sounded so serious.

"Isn't she something?" Chris asked after she left.

"Yeah, she's something." *As long as she was Chris's something.*

AMANDA'S CELL PHONE RANG, and she dashed downstairs from laying out her things for the gala at her mother's house, where they were getting ready together.

*It might be Eric.* She hadn't heard from him since his voicemail early this morning saying he'd arrived safely in Charleston. Had it only been this morning that he'd had to rush off. The phone stopped ringing. It seemed longer. She checked her call log. It had been Eric. Amanda pressed his number to return the call.

"Hey beautiful," he answered, knocking her a little off kilter.

"Hello handsome." She recovered.

"Miss me yet?"

"You've only been gone hours." *But I have been missing you.* "I am going to really miss you not being by my side this evening."

"The gala. I've been thinking of ways to make that up to you."

Amanda's imagination started a tingle that went from her head to her toes.

"Instead of offering a two-night, one-day trip to my next movie shoot as my contribution to the secret auction at the gala, ramp it up to five nights with three days on set and a chance to appear as an extra in the movie. What do you think? That should boost the bids."

"Ah, yes." She swallowed her disappointment. "But I was thinking more along the lines of personal ways to make that up to me."

"Darlin'," he drawled. "I don't have to do any thinking to come up with those."

Amanda fanned herself, thankful they weren't on a video call where he could see her flush. "Well, as long as you have that covered, how is Chris?" She resisted pointing out that he hadn't called her from the hospital.

"Not as bad as he could be. He had a concussion and broke his thigh, along with the expected scrapes and bruises. He's pushing to be released tomorrow, even though it's Sunday, and I hope we'll be on our way to Indigo Bay Monday. Early Tuesday at the latest."

"Let me guess. You don't want to miss our afternoon helping with the animal shelter open house and preadoption clinic."

"Right! That's it," he said dryly. Eric dropped his voice. "No, I don't believe I can last a minute longer than that without touching you. Repeatedly."

Amanda's mother's voice from upstairs interrupted her shudder.

"I'm finished in the bath," her mother shouted.

Eric laughed. "I think that's your cue. Before you go, there should be a little surprise arriving for you any minute."

"I'm at Mom's."

"I know. I texted your mom for your address. I never noticed the house number. She said you'd be at her place. The surprise is supposed to arrive before 8:00 when I'd planned to pick you up."

"I'm not a fan of surprises, but I'll make an exception for you."

"I plan to be the exception to any and all of your rules."

"Not over-confident, are we?"

"Babe, when it comes to you, it's all wishful bluster, not confidence."

The doorbell rang, and she jumped. "I've got to

get that. But if it helps, I love you and started missing you on the way home from Mom's last night."

"Of course that helps for a while until I can get another dose. Have fun. I'll leave you a good night message and talk with you tomorrow. I love you. Bye."

Amanda stared at the phone screen until the doorbell rang again. Then she answered the door.

"What have you got there?" her mother asked as she opened the package that had been delivered.

"A surprise from Eric." Amanda opened the florist box and lifted a corsage of small red flowers.

"Beautiful," her mother said. "I think they're lava burst orchids."

"I love them, whatever they are." Amanda noticed something else in the box as she started to put the corsage back in. "Oh," was all she could say as she lifted the red Cartier box, opened it, and saw the delicate white gold Love bracelet displayed on black velvet. "He shouldn't have. It might be the most beautiful piece of jewelry I've ever seen."

"Honey, it is gorgeous. And your teardrop filigree silver earrings will be perfect with it and your dress. You'd better scoot back upstairs and get ready yourself, or we'll be more than fashionably late."

A half-hour later, Amanda took one last look in the mirror. She hadn't wanted to go shopping with Sonja but was so glad she had. She absolutely loved the one-shouldered gown she'd found. The soft green fabric shot with silver threads hugged her figure without looking tight and the above-the-knee side slit gave the skirt enough play to shimmer when she walked.

"Oh," her mother said, as she walked into the living room. "You look lovely, and once you add the corsage Eric sent, I think you'll match the Gala color scheme perfectly."

That hadn't exactly been her plan, she'd simply fell in love with the dress. "Thanks." She spun around.

"Let me help you with the corsage and bracelet and I'll take a picture for you to text Eric."

"I thought you were in a hurry to leave."

"I can spare a minute or two for love."

Amanda went still while her mother pinned the orchids to her dress. Was she that obvious? She relaxed. What did it matter? This was Mom. She held her arm out for the bracelet, stepping back when her mother finished and crossing her hands in front to showcase the bracelet in the picture.

"I'll use my phone," her mother said, "so I have a copy." She snapped a few photos and tapped the screen a couple times. "I sent it to you. I'll drive, so you can text Eric on the way."

Amanda smiled and followed her out. *Yep*, Mom had allowed her a minute or two. She looked at the pictures and picked the one she liked best to text to

Eric. She was glad she'd stuck with wearing her hair down as she'd planned to for him.

*I adore the bracelet and orchids! Thank you. Sending a pic of me all ready to leave.*

His text came right back.

*I adore YOU! Thanks for the picture. But I'll need a private showing when I get home.*

Amanda warmed as much at Eric saying home as she did at the thought of a private showing for him.

*I might be able to fit that in my busy holiday schedule.*

*You do that and look for my goodnight later. Bye, love.*

"We're here."

Her mother's voice broke her fixation on Eric's text and brought her back into the present. Amanda glanced around as she got out of the car. Vehicles were already parked along the lengthy driveway, but not up to Seaside Boulevard yet. But it was still early, despite her mother's plan to arrive fashionably late.

She caught her breath when they walked into the B&B ballroom. The room had been pretty when she'd been in earlier in the day, but with the white Christmas lights the main illumination, it literally sparkled. Amanda laughed.

"What do you find humorous?" her mother asked.

"You are absolutely right. I match the decoration color scheme: forest green and silver with red accents."

"But you don't blend into the background."

"I should hope not." Amanda grinned. "Now, if you're good on your own, I'm going to get a drink and do some mayoral mingling."

"Try to have some fun, too."

"The same to you. No standing off in the corner by yourself."

"I intend to. Have fun, that is."

Amanda headed toward the bar. It was good to see Mom out of her shell. Once she had her drink, she made her way to the front of room, pausing to greet and talk with people on the way. She looked over the variety of silent auction items, from the motor scooter donated by Clint Walker, to a fabulous painting by Hope Ryan, to Eric's trip. Her stomach tensed. It still had the old description because she hadn't made a new one to bring with her.

She flagged down Sonja. "Can I use your computer. Since Eric couldn't make it tonight, he's sweetened his giveaway a lot. It should bump up bids."

"Let me get Gina. She did the signs." Sonja waved to Gina.

Amanda explained the situation and said, "Let's go to Sonja's front desk office and I'll write the information down for you." While Gina booted the computer, Amanda wrote Eric's new giveaway information on a piece of printer paper. "Thanks so much," she said, handing the information over and returning to the ballroom and the front table.

The band was on break, so she took the microphone from its stand. "Hi, everyone. Having a good time?"

The smaller than she'd expected crowd murmured "yes." Or maybe she was misjudging the number of people.

"I have an announcement. Two, in fact. Eric Slade is unable to attend the gala. His son had a skiing accident, and he's with him. His son's okay."

A hum went through the room.

"But Eric expects to be back for the animal shelter open house on Tuesday, and to make up for his not being here tonight, he's changing his secret auction prize from two nights and one day at his next movie shoot to four nights and three days at the shoot site plus the opportunity to be an extra in the movie. That also includes your transportation to and from the shoot. So everyone get up here and get your bid in on that and all the other great prizes we have for you. It all benefits the Indigo Bay Animal Shelter."

Amanda started to return the microphone to the stand and stopped. "A reminder. The silent auction bidding ends at 11:00, so the fundraising committee has time to determine the winners and announce them before midnight. If you're not here to claim your prize, a committee member will notify you by Monday." She handed the microphone over to the band, who'd returned from their break.

Lucille accosted her before she got three steps into

her mission to get a refill on her drink and one or more of the delicious-looking deserts on the side tables. She hadn't had much of a supper.

"I'm sorry about Mr. Slade not being able to be here," Lucille said. "Are you sure about his son. I haven't seen anything about that on Facebook or Twitter."

"I'm sure, Lucille." Amanda was relieved when Dallas tapped her shoulder and asked her to dance.

She spent the next couple of hours with a smile pasted on her face, socializing and missing Eric every time the band played a slow song. Her heart went out to Ariana Carol, a local singer trying to make a comeback, who'd sung a beautiful solo to an unexpected ending. A rescue dog had broken loose and ran onstage, followed by Ari's date, whose rescue had knocked them both to the floor, injuring Ari's arm.

Finally, it was time to announce the silent auction winners. Amanda took the microphone and list from Kittim Lane, the fundraiser's accountant and gala hostess, who'd quieted the crowd for her. Her heart sank when she skimmed the list and saw the winning bids. The amounts for the big items like the motor scooter and Eric's prize were lower than she'd hoped —no, expected.

She cleared her throat. "Drum roll please."

The band's drummer obliged.

Amanda announced the winners.

"Congratulations, all. If you're here, you can make arrangements with Kittim tonight to claim your prize. The others will be notified Monday. And let's have a hand for everyone who donated an item to the auction." She joined the crowd and scanned the room for her mother. Her duty was done. She was ready to go home and, she hoped, catch Eric's call. It was only 10:15 in Jackson Hole. She needed to hear his voice.

When she turned on her phone to take it off do not disturb, she saw Eric's text.

*Sorry, I couldn't wait until later. I'm done in by the time zone change and all and didn't want to break my promise to say goodnight.*

Amanda sniffed as she continued reading.

*Goodnight, love. Sweet dreams.*

She touched her finger to her lips before she texted back.

*Sweet dreams of you. Goodnight.*

# CHAPTER 14

Eric took the least time possible to drive a rental car from Charleston and clean up from his red eye private flight. He couldn't wait a moment longer to see Amanda. Touch her.

He bounded up the steps to her cottage, knocked, and let himself in when he saw Amanda in the living room. "Surprise!"

"Eric. You're early. We don't have to be at the shelter until one."

His gaze drank in her hair, makeup, long-sleeved t-shirt, his bracelet, and jeans. "I couldn't wait another second to see you. Besides, it looks like you're all ready to go."

"Guilty. I was dressed to go a half hour ago."

With that, he strode to her, took Amanda in his arms, threaded her hair through his fingers, and whispered in her ear, "Then why don't I mess you up a little and you can kill the rest of the time putting yourself back together while I watch?"

She snorted. "What girl could say no to an offer like that?"

He crushed his lips to hers and took the sustenance he'd been deprived of for three days.

They arrived at the animal shelter a little after 1:00. A woman hurried over to meet them.

"Eric," Amanda said. "This is Violet Montgomery. She and her husband Sterling run the Happy Paws Pet Shop and are heading the fundraising committee. Violet, Eric Slade."

"Nice to meet you," he said. "Did my publicity people get the photos to you?"

"Nice to meet you, too. And yes, we received the photos for you to autograph. But I think your idea of the in-person photos with you are going to be the bigger donation draw."

"Anything I can do to help. But I think I have some stiff competition. He nodded toward Santa Claus with a little girl and a kitten having their photo taken.

"Only with the younger set," Violet assured him. "Do you want a quick tour before you get down to work?"

Eric took Amanda's hand and wove his fingers between hers. "Sure."

Violet mouth turned up in a knowing smile. He

didn't care. Amanda squeezed his hand, sending a hum through him. Even better, she didn't, either.

Violet finished the tour and left them at the corner designated by a sign with a blown-up publicity photo of him. A donation box sat on a small table next to the easel with his picture.

"Are you a dog or cat person?" Amanda asked.

He sat in one of the two chairs set up. "Dog, I guess. I've never had a cat. Not that I have anything against them."

"Good. Because I'm going to adopt one. I lost my Miss Fluff this summer."

"I'm sorry." Why hadn't he known she had a cat. Simple. Before this trip they'd always gotten together in public places. He'd never seen her cat. There was so much he didn't know about her. Their gazes caught, and she sucked in a breath. And he wanted to know it all.

Amanda cleared her throat. "Thanks. She was 15. I'd expected it. But she'd been with me since I'd finished college."

"Let's pick one out before we leave."

"I'd like that," she said.

"But I'll help you with a better name than Miss Fluff."

She made a face and stuck out her tongue. Eric was thankful their first customer showed up then before he'd gone with his inclination to lean over and kiss her.

The afternoon flew by with Violet being right on the money that more people would want Amanda to take photos of him and them, with or without a potential pet, on their cell phones.

"We'd better look at the cats before the clinic's over," he said, when there was a lull in photo traffic. "Do you want a kitten?"

She shook her head. "The kittens are cute, but I'd rather take a young adult cat that's lost its owner. Usually, there's no problem finding homes for the kittens."

As they walked into the cat room, one cage immediately drew his eye. "Panther," he said as he strode over, taking Amanda with him. The cage held a pure black cat with the sinewy moves of a panther.

"Panther?"

"I'd forgotten. When I was about ten, the guy in the apartment next store had a cat like that named Panther. He and mom let me go over sometimes and play with Panther. We couldn't have a pet because that would have raised the rent. Mom always tried to get us the best place she could for what she could afford."

A volunteer came over before he could continue his blather. "Like him? This is a brother-sister pair that we'd like to place together."

Eric hadn't noticed the other cat, a furry butterball of a calico, that couldn't look more opposite of her sleek brother. "Can you take them out for us?"

The volunteer obliged, handing him the brother and Amanda the sister. Both broke into a purr in their arms.

"What do you think?" he asked.

Amanda dewy gaze was focused on him, rather than either of the cats. "Hmm?" She petted the cat in her arms.

"What do you think," he repeated,

"Where do we fill out the papers?"

While Amanda took care of the paperwork, Violet took photos of him with a couple last people waiting for pictures.

"All set." Amanda joined him. "We can pick them up next week, after Christmas." She hesitated. "Are you planning on taking Panther back to California? I can keep him, and you can pick him up after your skiing with Chris or whenever."

"No, I'm not taking him. They're a set, like us." He placed his hand on the small of her back and walked to the door. "I wouldn't split them."

Her smile was more dazzling than the bright winter sun shining on them when they stepped outside.

"What are you doing now?" he asked.

"I was going to help Sonja take down the ballroom decorations, but she decided to leave them up for the small New Year's Eve party she's having for her guests and a few friends. So I'll just be joining you and her and Jeff for supper."

"Followed by that private showing of your gala gown."

"If you behave."

He assumed a superior expression. "I always behave. Just sometimes better than others."

"Exactly."

"I'll walk you home, and then I'm moving my stuff back to the B&B for Chris's arrival tomorrow. He wanted to recuperate at the condo for a couple days, so he's gone back to his original plan to come Christmas Eve.

"I'm so glad he can still come."

"Me, too. Chris, Jeff and Sonja, you." He cleared his throat and tightened his arm around her waist. "It's the first family Christmas I've had in a good long time."

"And Mom. Don't leave her out." She squeezed him closer.

"Right."

"Why don't you go ahead to her house. I should be able to find my way home."

He gave her a peck on the lips when they came to their parting place. "I suppose not seeing you home is okay. It does limit my opportunities to lose good behavior points."

"Go." She pushed his shoulder and laughed.

The tinkle of her laughter stayed with him all the way to her mother's house.

LUCILLE WAS WAITING for her when Amanda reached her cottage.

"I have to talk with you," she called.

Amanda groaned. She'd just seen her at the animal shelter adoption clinic where Lucille had been fussing about the fundraising activities and amount raised. She didn't need more doom and gloom. Not after her disappointment with the silent auction proceeds and Kittim saying the gala committee was having trouble getting hold of the winner of Eric's prize—the highest bid of the evening. The winner was someone from out of town, and the second highest bid was significantly lower. She didn't know yet how the adoption clinic had fared.

Amanda mustered her patience. "We can sit on the deck." Amanda let the older woman and her Princess up the stairs. "I'll get us a drink." That would allow her to put up her mayoral complaint guard, too.

When she returned to the deck, Lucille had two magazines laid out on the table.

"I didn't want to say anything to you in public at the adoption clinic, but it's as I suspected from the start." Lucille punched her finger to a picture in one of the magazines. "Eric Slade has been toying with you, dear."

Amanda breathed deeply and counted to three. She'd asked Eric to run any publicity by her first before letting his PR people release it. She looked at the picture. This wasn't official PR. It was a shot that was part of a collage titled "Spotted this Weekend." She fingered her bracelet from Eric and checked the other magazine.

The same shot. Of Eric and Maya. Her heart splintered. They were in a jewelry store. He was slipping an engagement ring on her finger. Smiling, the smile she thought of as her smile.

Her cell phone rang. She took it out and glanced at the screen. A spam call, but Lucille didn't need to know that. "Sorry, I have to take this." She fled into the cottage, dropped onto the couch, and waited until she heard Lucille descending the steps. Then she burst into tears. She'd trusted him. Loved him. It was all fake. Their fake holiday romance was nothing more than that. For Eric, at least. She'd genuinely believed that he was his real self with her, and that he loved her. But it had all been an act.

An idea popped into her head. She gathered what pieces of her heart she could and went online. She wanted to resurrect some hope that she was overreacting. That the pictures were wrong. His official social media account didn't have anything confirming or denying it. All his fan club groups had the picture posted.

*Maya's accounts.* She'd have something if it were true, wouldn't she? Posts were sparse, but she did have one from the weekend that said, "TEASER! Look for some big news from me soon." It didn't have a picture.

Amanda went to Chris's account. Again, posts were few, except for a new one: "Out of the hospital with plans to celebrate the holidays with my dad. Expect a big announcement afterwards." The accompanying photo showed Chris leaving the hospital with Eric and Maya.

Her head pounded. Now she wouldn't have to lie to Sonja when she said she wasn't feeling well and couldn't make it for supper. After she texted Sonja, Amanda took some headache medicine, put on some soothing, music, and stretched out on the couch. Why did he do it? She'd agreed to the friendly fake romance and would have kept it to that if he'd been honest. His betrayal went far beyond blowing up her feelings. It could affect her friendship with Sonja since Eric and Jeff were so close. And what about her mother?

The headache medicine took effect and stilled her swirling thoughts. But not before she admitted defeat in ever finding true love and vowed not to try again. She'd been happy single. She'd be happy again.

So why was "Right!" in Eric's voice mocking her as she finally fell asleep.

"HI, BEAUTIFUL," Eric said as Amanda rustled and opened her eye.

She bolted upright. "You! How did you get in? And what are you doing here?

He gave her a moment to be fully awake before speaking. "The door was open, and I wanted to see how you were feeling."

She rubbed her temples. "The pain's gone, but the headache is still here."

What was that supposed to mean? He reached to touch her forehead, see if she had a fever and was delirious.

Amanda batted his hand away. "I'm done being part of your little drama."

He straightened and raised his hands in surrender. "What drama?" *He* was getting a headache now from his confusion.

She took her tablet from the table, powered it up, and tapped the screen. "This drama."

When he saw the picture of him and Maya, his stomach churned, and he thought he might upchuck his supper. He should have known better than to have gone out in public with her. But when he'd shared his plan with Chris, his son had encouraged him.

He calmed his agitation enough to speak. "I can explain. We were…" How could he explain without lying or giving away—

"Of course you can," she interrupted his thought with a shot that carried enough angry force for him to feel the hit physically. "But I've had enough of your subterfuge, your holiday play."

"What?" he demanded, unable to keep his frustration at bay while trying to stomp out the dual fires of dread and hurt flaring inside him.

"One of your personas says something, and another contradicts it. I'm supposed to believe both. I thought I knew the game rules when we dropped the fake romance. When I foolishly let my heart get involved."

Let her heart get involved, as if she had control of it? He hadn't any control. When it came to loving Amanda, his heart had a power of its own that he couldn't subdue. But he wasn't going to tell her that, give her more advantage over him.

"You're a chameleon. I believed I knew the real Eric Slade but know now that I've never seen him."

Eric's angry frustration exploded. "You've seen him. You've just refused to accept him. If you had, you'd hear me out."

Amanda massaged her temples again with enough

pain in her expression that he almost pulled her up from the couch and into his arms to let physical closeness say what she refused to hear in words.

She lifted her head and assumed a posture and expression that looked as brittle as it was steely. "Our deal is done. You gave me what I wanted, help with the fundraising, and I gave what you wanted—a *fake* romance. Please leave and don't contact me for the rest of the time you're in Indigo Bay."

Eric shook his head. She hadn't given him what he'd wanted. He'd thought she had, but she'd just taken it away. Maybe if he left and cruised around, he could get his head back on straight and figure out how to fix this.

"Go!" she repeated.

He clenched and unclenched his fists. "One last thing. You know how I said I didn't know if I'd ever truly loved a woman?"

She blanched but not a muscle in her face moved.

"The way you just ripped my heart apart. I know now." He stormed out, slamming the door behind him, but paused on the deck for a couple minutes to see if she'd come after him.

She didn't, shredding his last bit of hope.

# CHAPTER 15

The next morning when Amanda quickly ran out of things to do at the cottage, she went to her city hall office. There was always busywork there she could use to keep her mind off what Eric had done to her. "And you to him," her conscience said. But what did it know? It hadn't ever been in love and been betrayed.

"Hi, Amanda," Tracey said with an expression on her face that was surprised and something more Amanda couldn't read.

"Good morning. I needed to check on a couple things before the tree lighting tomorrow." She brushed by Tracey. Had she seen the picture? Probably everyone in Indigo Bay had, thanks to Lucille's helpful sharing. Amanda knew the older woman meant well, and she should be glad she found out before she and Eric took things any further.

Amanda released a dry laugh. He was engaged to another women. How could they have taken things further? She sat behind her desk, turned on her computer, and called public works to check on the city tree lights, something she could have done from home.

"Hi, Mayor," the department head answered. "I know why you're calling. Those replacement light strings are guaranteed to arrive by end of day today. We can add them to the tree tomorrow morning and give it a final check."

"What time? I may stroll by to see them." She had time to kill tomorrow until the lighting, then only Christmas and the morning after before Eric would be off to Jackson Hole again with Chris.

"Sure. About 9:30."

"Okay." She hung up and found a few more things to do—among them checking Eric's official fan sites. The photo of him and Maya had been deleted on all of them. His doing? Her heart softened. But she stopped it. The photo not being on the sites didn't mean it didn't exist.

She rummaged around for work to fill the emptiness inside her. But the more she found and finished, the more the emptiness seemed to grow. Eric had become a big part of her life. Maybe she should have let him explain before she'd made her decision. As she reached for her cell phone to call him, she realized he'd be in Charleston now picking up Chris. She'd try him later if she felt the same. It could be a momentary weakening that would go away.

The phone rang under her hovering hand, sending her heart into a pitter-patter until she saw it was only Sonja. "Huh." What did she mean only? Sonja was one of her closest friends.

"Hello."

"Hello, yourself. Is there something you want share?" Sonja's question ended in a rising lilt.

*The picture*! No Sonja wouldn't be teasing her about that. "I don't think so."

"So you wouldn't be the reason Eric left after supper ostensibly to check on you and didn't return until this morning?"

Amanda's shoulders shook involuntarily. Not in the way Sonja was thinking.

"He barely had time to switch his bike for the rental car and go pickup Chris and Maya in Charleston."

Amanda's throat closed. "Maya came, too," she got out in an almost a normal voice.

"Yes, we had an extra room free in addition to the suite, so it was no problem."

Amanda's mind went to the possible rooming arrangements, and she missed whatever Sonja said next, catching only her, "If I don't see you at the tree lighting tomorrow, we'll see you and your mother for Christmas dinner."

"Yeah, see you then." She leaned back, head on the chair's headrest and closed her eyes. She'd forgotten that she'd accepted Sonja's invitation to Christmas dinner before Eric had even arrived. She pushed the chair back and stood. Being outside might help. She buzzed Tracey and said she was leaving.

The breeze off the bay felt good as she headed for her first stop. The Emporium, Miss Eulalie's candy shop. The older woman's shop was a fixture in Indigo Bay, selling the best homemade candies for miles around.

"Hi, Amanda, what can I get you today?" Miss Eulalie, herself, said from behind the counter.

"I need to fill three. No make that two Christmas stockings." Her plan had been to fill stockings for her mother, Eric, and Chris.

"Two stockings coming up."

"I mean one." The other candy was for her and might not make it to Christmas. Miss Eulalie showed her the stocking selections they had. Amanda picked one, along with all her mother's favorite candies and hers. Miss Eulalie packed them up, and Amanda turned to leave, her mood boosted by the store's cheery holiday decorations and Miss Eulalie's cheerful help.

The door opened and her mother's next-door

neighbor greeted her with the same expression Tracey had.

"Hi." Amanda brushed by her, her stomach sinking. It was pity. She set her mouth, all the joy of candy shopping gone, and marched toward her next destination. Indigo Bay Accounting.

"Good afternoon, Mayor," the office assistant said.

"Is Kittim available?"

"Yes, go right in."

Amanda felt, or thought she felt, the assistant's gaze drilling into her back as she walked to Kittim's office. She knocked and went in. "I was in the neighborhood and thought I'd pop in to check on the donations instead of calling. How are we doing?"

"Better since the open house. I hear you and Eric Slade were great."

Key word, *were.* "It was fun. I'm adopting two cats."

Kittim laughed. "You're the third volunteer who's told me they're adopting pets. Back to business, we still haven't received a response from the winner of Eric's prize. If we have to award it to the next highest bidder, do you think he might throw in the difference?"

"I don't know." The Eric she'd thought she knew would. "He's staying at the Mansion B&B if you want to check with him. Sonja will put you through to him."

"I'll do that. Do you want me to print you the latest report?"

"No just send it to my email. I'm off to get cat stuff."

"Have fun."

Amanda shouldn't have felt the relief she did that the assistant wasn't at her desk when she passed by on her way out. She shook her arms, but that didn't shake the uneasiness. Nor did the happy prospect of getting another cat … cats.

"Hi, I'll be right with you," Violet called out from where she was helping another customer when Amanda made her last stop at the Happy Paws.

She nodded and browsed the cat supplies.

A voice drifted from the next aisle. "I feel sorry for the mayor that he took advantage of her like that."

Another responded, "Maybe she knew all along. Look at her mother. You know the saying about apples not falling far from the tree."

Amanda swallowed the bile in her throat. "Violet. I just realized I need to be somewhere. Don't worry, I'll be back." She fled the store.

The feeling she'd been having. She recognized it. It was the same one she had when she'd visited her mother in Indigo Bay before she'd moved here herself. When Mom was caring for Amanda's birth father. A feeling of people staring, pitying her, judging her mother, talking about her. But she hadn't felt it after she'd moved here.

She took a route home along the empty beach. Her thoughts were so jumbled. She wanted to talk with someone. Amanda kicked a small piece of driftwood. Not her mother. Mom had loved a married man for years and had never voiced any regrets to her. Not Sonja. She was too close to Eric, and Amanda didn't want to put her in a spot.

Amanda glimpsed a starfish struggling its way to the sea on the wet sand. She gently picked it up and put it in the water. Staring at the wave pattern, she longed to have someone by her side to talk to. *Not someone. Eric.* Hope flared. He'd wanted to explain but she hadn't let him.

Stars twinkled in the dark winter sky with a promise of tomorrow. She'd talk with Eric. *Tomorrow.* After she unjumbled her mind and emotions. And had a chance to peel off her past fears of love.

If she wasn't already too late.

"BREAKFAST ENDED AT 10:00," Jeff gave Eric grief he didn't need when he walked into the breakfast room at the B&B.

He had enough grief already. "Coffee. Hot and strong will do me. You do still serve that 24/7?"

"We do." Jeff turned a mug right side up and

poured a cup from the carafe in front of Chris. "What's with you? You've been like a grizzly bear with a hangnail banging around here since you picked Chris up at the airport yesterday morning."

"Hey, it had nothing to do with me," Chris said.

Eric gulped half the mug. Saying he'd gotten more than five hours sleep total the past two nights would be generous. "No, it has nothing to do with you, son. It's me. You know Jeff, when you said not to do anything stupid to mess up me and Amanda?"

Jeff huffed. "You did stupid."

Eric finished the rest of his coffee and held the mug out to Jeff. "I did mega stupid." He looked around. "Where are Sonja and Maya?"

"Freshening the evergreen branches Sonja has all around the place."

"Good. I need some help, but not theirs."

"What *did* you do?" Jeff asked while Chris looked on avidly.

Eric rubbed his neck. "I took Maya with me to help shop for a Christmas present for Amanda and someone took a photo. It looked like Maya and I were together, and the present was for her. The picture got posted all over social media."

Jeff shrugged. "Did you tell Amanda that."

"You'd think. I tried Tuesday evening when she confronted me, but Amanda wouldn't let me explain." For reasons colored by her past, he'd understood after he'd cooled down. "She's not taking my calls and doesn't respond to my texts. I think she's blocked me."

"That's tough, Dad."

Chris had a better overview of the situation than Jeff did. But Eric needed Jeff's help without getting down and dirty about his and Amanda's relationship and how he'd let his insecurity get the best of him and feel she was rejecting him.

Eric fortified himself with more of his coffee. "I have a plan."

"Does it involve you telling her you were stupid?" Jeff asked. "That's my go-to. Flowers also help."

Chris laughed.

"Listen and learn, young man," Jeff said. "Maybe jewelry for mega stupid."

"He has that covered," Chris said putting his hand over his mouth when Eric frowned at him.

"My plan involves admitting my wrongs," Eric said to answer Jeff. "That's not where I need your help. I need you to come up with a way to get Amanda to stick around after the tree lighting this evening until people are done hanging around the tree."

"Can I bring Sonja in on that?"

Eric tightened his grip on the coffee mug. "If you must." He wanted as few people involved as possible. "Ask Amanda to meet you or Sonja at the tree at, what? Six? Will people be cleared out by then?"

"Should be."

"Chris, I need you and Maya as props."

"Wow, I've always wanted to be a prop."

"This is serious," Eric said in a too-stern voice he regretted as soon as his words were out.

"I know, Dad." Chris patted his shoulder. "I've never seen you so serious about a woman that you don't just let whatever roll off you."

"Yeah, I'm so serious, it scares me."

Chris snorted.

"You wait until it hits you." Jeff waved his finger at him.

Chris sobered. "I know. I'm afraid I'm halfway there."

"What else?" Jeff asked.

"I meet Amanda instead of you."

"And?" Jeff prompted.

"That's all you need to know."

*Because I don't know for sure where I'm going from there.*

AMANDA TAPPED the metal pie pan against her leg and rubbed her arm. It was 6:05. Where was Sonja? She didn't mind helping her out with the pan she needed because she'd broken one of her glass pie pans. But it was getting chilly with no coat, just her teal cashmere sweater dress and gray leggings. And frankly she wanted to get home, practice what she was going to say to Eric tomorrow when she could get him alone and call it a day so tomorrow would come before she lost her nerve.

She made one more round of the tree, noticing how the new lights brightened it—thankful that they'd arrived as expected—and stopped at her wish ornament she'd picked up at Coastal Creations last minute. It was a tradition for townspeople to hang ornaments on the municipal tree Christmas Eve morning or afternoon and make a wish. She had, and when she'd connected the plug lighting the tree, she'd felt a lightness in her chest. It could have been the awe of the decorated tree lit, but she was holding onto the belief that it signaled the granting of her wish.

Her gaze dropped to the ornament below hers. It looked like it must be one painted at Coastal Creations. Scalloped bands of red and green ran around the top and bottom of the bulb. In between bold black letter said, "BES & AJS" with a smaller, finer "Forever?" written below. Amanda's stomach flip-flopped. AJS were her initials. But she didn't know anyone with the initials BES. And the AJS could be someone else. Or she could have a secret admirer. She laughed. One admirer was more than she could handle.

"Like it?"

*Eric!* She took another look at the ornament before turning. His initials were ES. She didn't know his middle name. Her heart ignited as she faced him, but the spark fizzled when she saw Maya next to him. Amanda couldn't help it. She dropped her gaze to the young woman's left hand. *No ring.* Before her tightly strung emotions could process that, a motion to Maya's left drew her focus there. To Chris, who had Maya's hand firmly in his.

"I know my work is spectacular, but I didn't expect it to leave you speechless."

While his acting skill allowed him to pull off his comment in a teasing tone, his eyes were a study in uncertainty. Knowing she'd caused that uncertainty pinched her chest.

"Here." He tossed car keys to Chris, who glanced back and forth between her and Eric.

"Don't worry," she said. "I'll get him back for Christmas."

Chris raised an eyebrow in a fashion so like his father that she had to smile. He and Maya left hand-in-hand. She was going to have to ask about them. But more important things first.

She titled her head as if seriously studying his artwork. "You obviously put a lot of work into your ornament. I assume I'm AJS. You could be ES, but what's the B for? And why the question mark?"

Eric's chest puffed as if a weight had been lifted,

and she couldn't help reveling in the thought she had that power.

"Burton. As in Burton Cummings, lead singer of the Guess Who. Mom was a huge fan. I'm your man if you need a tutorial on their lyrics or ever need a partner for Guess Who trivia. In fact, I'm not bad at 70s rock trivia in general. Mom had second thoughts on her name choice when she heard people at daycare calling me Burtie. From then on, I was Eric. I legally changed my name to Eric Burton Slade when I started acting.

"I didn't know any of that."

"Not many people do, but I want you to know everything about me."

"And that partner stuff is especially interesting, but it's not trivia partnering I'm particularly interested in." Her words lifted the pounds of fear and uncertainty, her guilt about hurting him, and the baggage of her past and blew them away as if they were nothing. She shook with the giddiness of freedom from them.

"Here." Eric fumbled in his leather jacket pocket for something, then helped her on with it.

She snuggled into the soft lining, closing her eyes, and breathing in the scent of winter air and Eric. When she opened her eyes, he was on one knee holding an open ring box. "The ring in the picture," she whispered.

"Maya was helping me shop. I didn't want to

mess up. Get the wrong style. Wrong size. Something too ostentatious so you'd think I was trying to buy your love."

"Oh, Eric." Tears clogged her throat. "I wouldn't let you explain. I hurt you. Let you think I didn't know, love the real you." She went down on her knees in front of him. "I love the real Eric Slade, the fake boyfriend Eric Slade, the actor Eric Slade, and any others hiding in there." She poked his chest.

"And I understand why you shut me out," he said

Her eyes shined like beacons to him. Silently welcoming him into her heart.

"But can we talk about sorrys and all that stuff later? I'm getting so off script I'm in danger of losing it."

She sat back on her heels and gazed with love at the most wonderful, fascinating, loving, and confounding man she'd ever met. *Her man.*

"That look isn't helping." He swallowed. "Amanda Jade Strickland, I love you more than I fear I will ever be able to show you. Will you marry me?"

She held her hand out for him, her fingers ice cold. "Yes Burton Eric Slade, I love you as I've loved and will love no other. Yes, I'll marry you." He touched her hand and her fingers warmed as he slipped on the ring. Amanda stretched out her arm. "It's beautiful."

He stood and gave her a hand up. "You're beautiful. Merry Christmas."

"Merry Christmas." She lifted her face to him, and her gut wrenched. "I don't have a Christmas gift for you."

"You just gave me the best Christmas gift a man could ask for." He crushed her to him and sweetened that gift with the most searing kiss either of them could imagine.

# EPILOGUE

Amanda sat in the sitting room off the B&B's ballroom trying not to chip off the lovely rose manicure Indigo Bay Nails and More had squeezed her in for this afternoon. Both her mother and Sonja had initially thought a one-week engagement was crazy. But she and Eric couldn't wait.

Not after talking for much of the night Christmas Eve and after Christmas dinner with her mother and Chris and Maya at Jeff and Sonja's. They'd settled most everything from what to name the cats to where they'd live—her cottage, for now. Everything but who loved who more. They were leaving that a draw.

She and Mom and Sonja had pulled off the wedding planning with the help of her other Indigo

Bay friends and Eric's "connections." Sonja's small New Year's Eve party for her guests had been transformed into a wedding reception New Year's Eve open house with word-of-mouth invitations.

Amanda stood—not for the first time—smoothed the skirt of her gala gown, checked her reflection in the wall mirror, and adjusted the holly and mistletoe crown Sonja had cleverly fashioned for her in lieu of a veil.

"Wedding day jitters?" her mother asked. "If you have any doubts…"

"No doubts." The harpist, a friend of Eric's, started the wedding march, ending the conversation. Amanda picked up her bouquet of lava burst orchids. Eric again. She looped her arm through her mother's and followed her attendants, Sonja, her daughter Lauren, and Maya to the ballroom entryway.

Sonja had added a few touches to the gala decorations and, rather than rows of chairs, round and larger rectangular tables had been arranged on either side of an aisle. They all looked full, but Amanda didn't register any of the people who sat in them. She had eyes only for Eric, standing on the bandstand with the pastor of her and Mom's church and Jeff, his best man. When her attendants cleared and he could see her, his eyes widened and softened with love. Her knees went weak.

"Buck up, soldier," her mother said. "We're on."

Somehow she and Mom made it to the bandstand and up the steps.

"Who gives this woman in marriage?" the pastor asked.

"I do," her mother responded and released her hand to Eric.

When he took it, they smiled as one.

"Dearly beloved …" the pastor began, "… Amanda Jade Strickland, do you take Eric Burton Slade …"

She said her vows, tears streaming down her face by the time she finished with "I do."

Eric began his, projecting his voice as if he wanted the whole world to hear.

"In sickness and health, till death do you part?" The officiant looked at Eric.

Tears dampened her eye lashes. Eric had asked her if they could include that part of the traditional wedding vows, as if he needed to make one final affirmation to her of his love.

"I do!" he boomed.

"Then I pronounce you husband and wife. You may kiss the bride."

And kiss her, he did until a couple whistles and cat calls brought Amanda from the fog, and she ended the kiss.

He offered his arm and pulled her tight to his side. "I suppose we have to stay here for a while," he whispered.

"Behave," she whispered back.

"If I do, will I finally get that private showing you've been teasing me with?"

His gaze ran up and down her, causing a tingle that made her glad for his solid form beside her and strong arm to lean on.

"Oh babe, will you …"

**FROM JEAN C. Gordon:**

*It's a potent mix . . .*
A jilted bride and her ex's brother working on a Christmas puppy giveaway.

Add a matchmaking grandmother pushing a dating app, plus a wounded moose.

Will it spark a forever Christmas love or a disaster of broken trust?

**Find out in** my latest holiday story, ***Can't Say No to Puppies***, A Puppies for Christmas novella. At your favorite online bookstore.

**All My Other Holiday Romances**
Caro's Gift
A Team Macachek Christmas Anthology

Holiday Escape Novella
A Team Macachek Novella
Christmas Pizza to the
Rescue Novella

Sweet Complications by Stacy Claflin
Sweet Adventure by Tamie Dearen


INDIGO BAY SWEET ROMANCE SERIES
Sweet Saturday by Pamela Kelley
Sweet Beginnings by Melissa McClone
Sweet Starlight by Kay Correll
Sweet Forgiveness by Jean Oram
Sweet Reunion by Stacy Claflin
Sweet Entanglement by Jean C. Gordon
Sweet Dreams by Stacy Claflin
Sweet Matchmaker by Jean Oram
Sweet Sunrise by Kay Correll
Sweet Illusions by Jeanette Lewis
Sweet Regrets by Jennifer Peel
Sweet Rendezvous by Danelle Stewart


HOLIDAY SHORT READS
Sweet Holiday Surprise by Jean Oram
Sweet Holiday Memories by Kay Correll
Sweet Holiday Wishes by Melissa McClone
Sweet Holiday Traditions by Danielle Stewart


Missing some books from your collection?
Find out more about Indigo Bay at
www.sweetreadbooks.com/indigo-bay

For *USA Today* Bestselling author Jean C. Gordon, writing is a natural extension of her love of reading. From that day in first grade when she realized t-h-e was the word the, she's been reading everything she can put her hands on. Jean and her college-sweetheart husband share a 175-year-old farmhouse in Upstate New York with their daughter and her family. Their son lives nearby. Connect with Jean on Facebook, as @JeanCGordon on Twitter, or on JeanCGordon.com.

## ALSO BY JEAN C. GORDON

Thank you for reading my story. I hope you enjoyed it and all the other Indigo Bay stories you've read. Don't miss out on any of my new releases. Sign up for my READERS GROUP NEWSLETTER to receive news about me, promotions, and giveaways. And I always appreciate when my readers take the time to leave an honest review of my books.

(Meet teenage Jesse and Lauren)
Holiday Escape
A Team Macachek Christmas
(Prequel to Sweet Entanglement)
Christmas Pizza to the Rescue
A Team Macachek Christmas Anthology
(All three holiday novellas: Holiday Escape, A Team
Macachek Christmas and Christmas Pizza to the
Rescue)

UPSTATE NY...WHERE LOVE IS A LITTLE
SWEETER
Bachelor Father
Love Undercover
Mandy and the Mayor
Candy Kisses
Mara's Move

LOVE INSPIRED
FRESH-START FAMILIES
Reuniting His Family
A Mom for His Daughter
THE DONNELLY BROTHERS
Hometown boys make good…and find love
Winning the Teacher's Heart
Holiday Homecoming
The Bachelor's Sweetheart

ANTHOLOGIES

THE MATCHMAKERS
A Match Made in Williamstown